PRAISE FOR *FALLING THROUGH SPACE:*

"This rollicking space adventure tale unfolds with great imagination and humor. Fast-paced storytelling entertained me as I thoroughly enjoyed the lively characters and twists and turns of plot."

—Liz Morton Duckworth, author of *Poker Alice Tubbs: The Straight Story*

"…a fun mix of soap opera, love story, first contact, and solar-system exploration that pokes fun at bureaucracy, academia, and relationships."

—John E. Stith, author of *Manhattan Transfer*

"The story moves like gangbusters, packed with twists, wit, and laughs. It's sci-fi that doesn't take itself too seriously but still delivers the goods. The author clearly has a good head, a good heart, and a slightly warped imagination (the best kind). Perfect for readers who want both substance and a good time."

—Dean S.

"Much like Becky Chambers' *Monk and Robot* and *Wayfarers* series, and Andy Weir's *Project Hail Mary, Falling Through Space* provides an engaging imagining of life beyond human experience and the potential for unlikely friendships. Here's to green skinned, tentacled, and robot friends and finding ways forward, especially when we feel like we are falling."

– Sarah K.

"Definitely not predictable. Humor that fills every nook and cranny like applesauce on white carpet. Rich personalities, even aliens, page turner, like an itch you can't reach. More please."

—Bill S.

"…fast-paced, full of surprises, and seriously fun.…sharp story-telling with heart and humor."

—Nadine Keaney, Front Row Entertainment

"Smart, witty and fun, and easily accessible for those us who appreciate sci-fi but aren't experts in astronomy. I especially enjoyed the quick banter and well-written dialogue between the characters!"

—Kailey H.

"Like fine wine.… written with passion and attention to detail with just the right number of flavors to want more."

—Bonnie F.

FALLING THROUGH SPACE

A NOVELLA

MICHAEL L. STEVENS

Falling Through Space

A Novella

Jolibro Publishing
www.jolibro.com
info@jolibro.com

Visit the author @ www.michaellstevens.com

Paperback: ISBN 978-1-953474-12-4
eBook: ISBN 978-1-953474-13-1

Library of Congress Control Number: 2025942844

FALLING THROUGH SPACE

A NOVELLA

MICHAEL L. STEVENS

Jolibro

La Mesa, California

This book is dedicated to Linda, who inspired;
to Bill, who encouraged;
and to Lianne, who realized.

WIZARDRY

The starship *DE PROFUNDIS* winked into existence close to Earth. It sped down on a trajectory that would take it much closer, touching even the outer molecules of the Earth's atmosphere. (The phrase "winked into existence," however, is probably unfair to *De Profundis,* since it can hardly be said that a half-mile-wide chunk of rock doesn't always exist at least *somewhere.* Still, the operators of *De Profundis* refused to disclose where the ship had really been prior to its winking-in, declaring such information to be proprietary. They had, early on, decided that the truth—"we don't know how it works"—would unfortunately sound too much like the Wizard of Oz.)

So: the starship winked into existence and prepared for another close pass, closer even than the one it had made the month before. It plunged grimly down to yet another Earth welcome, which consisted of panicked news reports, riots at embassies, and even a ballistic missile arcing up out of the atmosphere.

The *De Profundis* neatly side-stepped the missile (more winking) and boosted it into higher orbit where it would cause no harm by falling back. Since the ship would no doubt be blamed for any terrestrial damage caused by an errant missile, it was deemed best to pretend it never happened.

The governments of Earth, most of whom were planning to steal or destroy the *De Profundis* while at the same time contracting with it to haul scientists, cargo, and supplies to their bases on the Moon and Mars, tacitly agreed to this fiction.

CHAPTER 1

●

ROADRUNNER

Flynn Hopper studied the map on his phone. "Take a left at the next light," he said. The car turned, cruised past an older McDonald's and a small used-car dealership, then proceeded down an unpromising street lined with warehouses.

A voice from the back seat asked, "Are you sure, Flynn?" It was Professor Carolyn Parks, to whom Flynn was Graduate Assistant. As always, she looked very business-like in her crisp, pinstriped suit. As always, she was checking his results.

"That's what the GPS says," replied Flynn.

"This is ridiculous," said Professor Lonigan. He was gray-haired, imposing, and the Head of the Department. He drove on in silence for a few moments.

"There it is on the left, where those people with signs are standing in the street." Flynn pointed.

Lonigan turned into the driveway of a dingy-looking brown brick structure. It looked like there might be parking in rear, but a heavy iron gate blocked their passage. A man in vaguely military-looking garb walked over from his task at the front of the building. His nametag read *Schwarz*. Flynn lowered the window.

"You here for the Day Pro?" the man asked.

"*De Profundis*," corrected Professor Lonigan. He had taught for many years.

"Whatever. You got tickets?"

Flynn showed the code on his phone. Schwarz scanned it with a tablet, looked at his screen, studied their faces, and made an arm gesture. The gate opened. "Park in the rear," he said.

Flynn looked at what the man had been doing, which appeared to involve a thick canvas hose. "Are you planning to put out a fire?" he asked.

"Yup. Now let's move it. You're the last to arrive."

Schwarz followed their car into the lot and waited while they parked. "Do you have luggage?" he asked.

"Yes, thank you," replied Professor Lonigan. "You'll find it in the trunk."

"Good," said Schwarz. "Stack it on the loading dock over there. We'll check it later." He went off to chain the gate.

In the end, of course, it was Flynn who did the stacking. The professors, who frequently travelled to conferences, owned stylish suitcases. It made Flynn feel a little ashamed of his own pack, a duffle bag he'd found at the Army Surplus store. It had "Smith" stenciled on it, but it looked serviceable. It was all he could find at the last minute.

Professor Emerick, who'd been a mentor to Flynn, had raised the funds and made the arrangements for this expedition, but he died suddenly. Flynn was tagged as a last-minute replacement. He couldn't really argue with his good fortune.

If, in fact, it *was* good fortune.

Please don't go, Louise had begged.

If I don't go, what will we do?

I'll finish my student teaching at the School for the Deaf and Blind she'd said. *You'll write your doctoral thesis. We'll be fine.*

Do you know what my thesis advisor wants me to write about? 'Exothermic Inelastic Scattering of Twisted Magnetic Ropes in BY Draconis Variables.' It doesn't float my boat. I mean, twisted magnetic ropes have been done to death already. How could there be anything new to discover, even in BY Draconis Variables?

How indeed? she'd asked in mock surprise. *And that's your problem. You're just like Boots.*

Do you mean Boötes? He pronounced all three syllables.

No, I mean Boots. She was my dog when I was young and she was an inveterate explorer. When we went walking, she'd zig and zag across the trail, exploring over here, then over there. She always had to run up to the top of the next hill, just to see what was there. That's you.

I guess you're right. That is me. But think about it: If I go on this trip, I'll get lots of material to write about. I can finish my thesis, we can get married, we'll both get teaching positions, and we can buy a house instead of renting an apartment.

Wait a minute, she'd said, *what was that part about getting married?*

"You gonna stand there all day?" Schwarz looked down at him from the dock.

"Sorry."

"Gimme your stuff, kid. We're running late. In fact, the sooner we're out of here the better I'll like it."

"Are you expecting trouble?"

"Seems like there always is. Nothing we can do about it, either, except move fast."

"Yes, sir. I'll try."

"You don't have to call me 'sir'. First, I'm not an officer, and second, we're not in the military. We just act like it."

"Sorry sir."

"Call me Ernie." He was an old man, maybe forty at least, thin, wiry, and as pale as if he'd been away from the sun for a long time—which he had, of course. Still, there was something in his eyes that told you not to mess with him.

"I'm Flynn."

"Fine kid. Now get going—you're late for the meeting."

The other passengers, thirty or forty of them, stood grouped around a guy who certainly looked like a ship's officer, who was saying, "… so welcome aboard the *De Profundis*, and to the first manned expedition to the outer planets." Faint applause. "Second, we apologize for the confusion, but we don't have time to explain a lot right now. Please just do as we ask, and we'll tell you more after we leave the planet. For now, just understand that the ship will make only one more pass by Earth and that we've got operations to accomplish all over the globe during that tight timeframe."

"Sort of like Santa Claus," observed Flynn.

A few people laughed. A few stared. The officer scowled in Flynn's direction. "Yes," he said at last, "that's right: just like Santa Claus. So, when I tell you to move your ass you will move it, and when I tell you to jump—which I WILL do—you will jump. Do I make myself clear?"

"Yes sir," said Flynn.

"Good. Now, the current ship's time is…seventeen thirty-six hours. Set your watches. The Transfer will take place from eighteen fifty-five to nineteen oh five. In the meantime, we're going to split you up. Last names starting A through M will report for gear-check. Last names N through Z will report to chute training."

The old warehouse wasn't big, but its emptiness made it look bigger. Flynn noticed some dusty display stands scattered around and a few trampled greeting cards on the floor. The whole place exuded an end-of-season/imperfect-seconds sale feeling.

Standing in line, Flynn texted, *"Heading to Outer Space in an hour. I love you."*

She sent, *"I love you back. So stay away from those green-skinned women!"*

He sent, *"Ok no green skin. But I've also got a thing for tentacles."*

She sent, *"You come here lover, and I'll show you tentacles."*

He sent a smiley face.

Gear-check required opening luggage and throwing out unnecessary items like suits, ties, and weapons. Casual clothes, books, electronics—even chocolate and booze—were allowed. Then the items were re-packed into ship's bags. (It turned out Flynn's duffle was okay after all.) The bags were loaded into bins, and the bins were lifted onto a conveyor belt. The belt wasn't moving, however. It just ended above a bare spot on the floor.

Chute training turned out to consist of scaffolding that held up a set of curtains. At the top of the stairs Flynn found a hole in the scaffold floor, below which dangled black netting – the chute. "This looks like playground equipment," said Flynn.

"Yup," said the crewman there, "with a few modifications." He raised his voice: "Listen up! Has anybody here ever jumped off a diving board? Good. Well, you know that little hop you take just before the dive? I want you to do the same thing here, only this time, at the end of the hop, you go down the chute. Got it? I hope so. Now the thing is, you grounders always bang your pretty little faces on the far side of the chute. Trust me, you don't want to do that. So, you WILL wear helmets with faceplates while you're jumping, and you'll keep on jumping until you don't bang your face anymore. Any questions?"

There were no questions. Flynn needed only one jump before they sent him off to report to Schwarz. Lonigan was still jumping a half hour later and looked tired. "Don't worry," said Ernie. "There's always at least one. They'll have him go first and make him sit on the edge. It's only later, when things get tight, that you want a quick jump."

"Why? What happens later?"

"Oh, you know, excitement, tensions, things like that. Speaking of which, I need you to help me out front with the hose."

"Are we putting out fires?"

"No, we're putting out people. They found us early this time. That's never good."

There were more protestors in the street now, and they were yelling things that didn't sound nice. Some hollered about terrorism. Some held forth about violating God's Law. Some were dressed in costumes from every sci-fi show Flynn had ever seen and others he hadn't. Those folks seemed most upset about not being invited along. Flynn, who had been added at the last minute, grinned smugly at them. Fortunately, nobody noticed.

Some people yelled about ruining the environment. Some yelled about endangering Earth with a space rock the size of the one that wiped out the dinosaurs. Flynn thought those folks had a good point. And then a single, black-and-white sign rose above the crowd, with just two hands holding it up. *Solve the Omega Problem,* it said.

Flynn stood still, staring at it…until Ernie elbowed his ribs and told him to pay attention. Some people were throwing things. Ernie and Flynn sent a jet of water in that direction to back them off. The police showed up, but they only watched.

The standoff continued for what seemed like hours. At last Ernie yelled, "It's eighteen forty-five kid. Get inside!"

"What about you?"

"I'll be along. Now go."

Flynn saw that most of the ship's crew were attending to the conveyor belt. The officer was addressing the passengers. "Ladies and gentlemen, we're about to board the ship."

"Are you going to beam us up like Scottie?" Flynn asked.

The officer scowled in Flynn's direction again and this time recognized him. "No, Mr. Hopper, we are not. Do you really want your body broken down into billions of atoms and then hope that a computer can put you back together in the right order?"

"Uh, no," replied Flynn.

"Of course not. We'd never use anything as ridiculous as a 'transporter.' No, instead we're going to use the Roadrunner Method." He held up a circle of black cloth.

"Oh crap," said Flynn.

"What's the Roadrunner Method?" whispered Dr. Parks.

"My guess: you paint a tunnel on the side of a rock," answered Flynn. "You run through the tunnel. Wile E. Coyote tries to follow and slams into the rock."

"Oh crap," said Dr. Parks.

"It's actually a little more complicated than that," said the officer, who'd evidently overheard. He laid the circle on the floor and pointed a controller device at it. He began making adjustments.

"Still," said Flynn, "it could be analogous to a white hole, on a small scale at least."

"But where's the power source?" asked Dr. Parks.

"Obvious fakery," said Professor Lonigan. "That much energy would fry us all."

"True," said Dr. Parks, "but in light of our hypothesis about the ship's drive, a spatial tunnel is worth considering."

"Dr. Lonigan!" called the officer. "We've established contact. We're in standby mode. Could you come here, sir?"

They did indeed direct Lonigan to sit on the edge of the cloth and—amazing! —his legs dangled down into the blackness below. Small gasps arose from the passengers. Yells and screams came from the street outside.

"Synch!" shouted the officer. "Ready and…go!" Lonigan slid (or was pushed) into the hole. The other passengers followed, hopping up, sliding down, some bumping their faceplates. Then the conveyer belt moved, dropping food, fuel, water, supplies, and finally baggage into the tunnel. The crew ran up to the officer, who counted them as they dropped through. He then nodded at Flynn and jumped himself.

Flynn looked around at the empty warehouse. He glanced at his watch. It said nineteen oh three—oops—nineteen oh four. He heard more yelling from outside. He heard a door crash open. Ernie appeared, running hard, with a crowd in hot pursuit. "Jump, kid!" he yelled. Flynn jumped.

Ernie leapt high and, with practiced precision, centered himself on the hole, grabbed the edge of it as he passed through, and dragged it in after himself. The crowd, screaming wildly, fell on the place where he'd been a moment before—and slammed into the bare floor.

CHAPTER 2

●

LUNACY

Flynn slid downward through the chute. It was funny, he thought, sliding Down to go to a place that was obviously Up. It had to be a convenient property of spatial tunneling. He remembered what the chute crew member had said: "You'll come out into a zero-gravity cave, and you'll still have momentum. Don't worry. We've got a padded funnel to catch grounders." He looked at Flynn and added, "Crew always grab the shrouds. Try for those if you can."

Flynn burst out of the chute and glided into a vast cavern that was dark but crisscrossed by the beams of spotlights. He saw his fellow passengers gliding ahead, beyond his feet. The funnel must be that way. He looked to the sides of the cavern and saw a netting that curved like a spider's web, narrowing to the width of a single rope at the center, where he was drifting. He reached out, missed it with his hand, but caught it in his left elbow. That converted his forward momentum to rotational. He gritted his teeth and struggled to hold on. The net imparted a twisting motion that caused his feet to move outward, where they touched a wider part of the shroud. It suddenly seemed to him that there *was* an up and down to the cave, and that he was dangling high above the—he guessed *deck* would be the right term.

Flynn crawled carefully down the shroud. As he stepped out of the last loop a woman, trailed by two children, ran toward him with open arms. He got out only a semi-intelligent, "Huh?" before a crew member pulled him aside. The woman slammed into the man who'd been just behind him on the shroud. The kids hugged his legs.

"Who's that?" Flynn asked.

"That's Enrique," said the crewman. "We couldn't go without him. He's the best cook we've got—makes a mean veggie burger out of that slush from Hydro."

"So, you're all allowed to bring family aboard?"

"Of course. We've got lots of family here. Still plenty of room, though." The crewman gestured overhead.

Flynn looked up and saw a small town suspended in the dark sky, complete with buildings, streets, and streetlights. He thought maybe if he went up in a small plane and flew over a small Iowa town in the evening, he might see something very much like that. He craned his neck and followed the line of the town around a great, curved wall—right down to the place he stood.

"It looks so…*Midwest*," he murmured.

The crewman smiled. "It sure does. We've even got a town square. Which, by the way, is where you're supposed to go for orientation and assignment. It's just two streets down and three over, so get going!"

"Where, exactly?"

"It's simple; you just…Forget it. I'll show you."

It took a while to get all the passengers gathered. Somebody said a man was caught in the funnel and needed help getting out. Flynn had an idea who that might be but didn't say anything.

•••

Captain Wagner welcomed everyone aboard but seemed anxious to finish with the formalities. He turned the meeting over to his subordinates, who herded the crowd through intake processing.

The guy behind the table looked up Flynn's name. "Here we go," he said. "You're in Unit Z33. That's in Uptown."

"Uptown?" replied Flynn. "Sounds swanky. Where's it at?"

"Look up," said the guy. "See the town? That's Uptown." It was dark in Uptown, nearly a half mile away, with a few lights showing.

"So," he asked, "then where we're standing is…?"

"Downtown. Right. The mess hall's over there. There'll be a reception at twenty-one hundred hours, so you've got time to stow your stuff and get back. Grab your bag from the pile over there and get going." Flynn picked up his bag and turned away.

"Hey!" the crewman yelled, "That's uphill. It's easier downhill." He pointed in the other direction. Flynn turned around and—yes— the bag felt lighter. Of course: the ship's rotation provided gravity. Going in the same direction as that rotation added weight. Going in the other direction removed weight. Walking from Downtown to Uptown and back, he could at least go downhill all the way.

The neighborhood around Z33 seemed sparsely populated.

He noticed a few lights scattered about but didn't see any people. The Unit wasn't too bad: a bit dusty but nice. He threw his stuff on the bed, used the bathroom (or was it the "head"?), checked out the kitchenette, and headed back downtown.

Flynn grabbed a drink of punch—which turned out to be non-alcoholic—and a sandwich at the reception, then looked around. Standing amid a small group, Professor Lonigan was leading a heated discussion about the Omega Problem. Flynn wandered over and listened for a while. There were strange things going on in the solar system, but there was no agreement in the room as to what they meant. At a pause in the debate Flynn said, "I've got a theory about that."

Lonigan looked around at him. "Really? That's fine, young man. I like to hear student theories. Send me your notes on it and I'll get back to you." He turned to his colleagues and picked up where he'd left off.

Flynn looked around. He saw Professor Parks coming his way and noted that she'd changed from her pin-striped suit into something more utilitarian. It was an off-khaki blouse and matching slacks with lots of pockets and shiny buttons, like a designer version of the crew uniforms. "Professor!" he called, "over here."

"Oh hi, Flynn," she said. "How are you doing?"

"I'm excited! And how about this ship? I mean, it's almost perfect. You've got rotation for gravity, and then the rock gives you protection from radiation, meteorites… Denebian slime devils… and such." He could see she wasn't listening.

"Yes, it's nice," she said.

"I wonder what the propulsion system is."

"I don't know, really. Umm, would you excuse me?" She moved to join Lonigan's group.

Flynn looked after her and shrugged. He remembered some interesting hors d'oeuvres he'd seen and wandered that way. A hand grabbed his shoulder.

"Come over here, kid. I got a table," Ernie said. "So," he added, "what's the matter? You don't look so happy."

"Nothing," Flynn replied, "it's just that…"

"You don't fit in with the academic crowd?"

Flynn laughed. "No, I *do* fit in. Only I fit at the bottom rung."

"I see. Here, drink up."

"Is it alcoholic?"

"No, not on the first night. Not until you've earned it."

"How do I do that?"

"Well, you know, everybody here gets a duty assignment. Some in maintenance, some in navigation, some in science, and so on."

"I'll bet I get assigned to peeling potatoes."

It was Ernie's turn to laugh. "Funny you should say that. You *were* on the KP roster."

"I was? You mean I'm not anymore?"

"Nope. I put you on my roster."

"What's that?"

"The Bosun crew."

"Boson? Sounds like an elementary particle."

"I wouldn't know about that. Bosun's an important part of the ship."

"Okay. I guess I'm honored then. When do I start?"

"First watch."

"When's that?"

"In one hour, from midnight to oh eight hundred. Come over to my office. It's one street up and two over. We'll get you a uniform."

The uniform turned out to be gray coveralls, black boots, and a gray hat.

"It's not very impressive," Flynn said.

"No, it isn't kid. Real work isn't impressive. It just needs to get done. Now let's get going. We're walking security tonight."

"Security? Do I get to wear a sidearm?"

Ernie stopped in his tracks, turned back. "Listen, kid: guns are dangerous. VERY dangerous."

"I know that."

"No, you don't. Listen to me. We don't allow guns on the ship at all. If you see one, don't touch it. Report it to me instead and I'll take care of it."

"Okay."

"And above all, never, ever, fire a gun on board this ship. You got that?"

"Yes sir."

"Don't call me…"

"Sir. I got that too."

"Good. Now let's go."

They walked up, they walked down, they walked around. Ernie pointed out locations as he told Flynn about policies, rules, and other Standard Operating Procedures.

Flynn asked, "I was wondering, do you know what the propulsion system is?"

Ernie said, "There ain't no propulsion, kid."

"So how does it…?"

"Move? It just falls. It's always falling."

"But…"

"But… the ship gets to pick where it's falling to."

"How do you mean?"

"Well, it's like, when you came aboard, we were falling toward the Earth, only falling in orbit. Then we decided to orbit the Moon, so we asked the ship to fall toward the Moon. It did, and now we're in lunar orbit."

"Wait a minute. The ship did it?"

"Yup. And that stuff's complicated. You gotta pick the right spot, avoid obstacles, add momentum or bleed momentum off, and so on. It usually takes a couple of tunnels to get the orbit right, but the ship knows how."

"It does? You mean, it has some sort of artificial intelligence?"

"More like it *is* artificial intelligence. It's darn smart, anyway. It must be to shunt us around space and not get lost."

"Does it talk?"

"Good question, but I don't know the answer. I said a thing once, and it responded by doing what I asked for, but I never heard it talk. Maybe it talks to the captain though."

"How do they navigate then?"

"Mostly they type it into machines in the command center."

"That's really old-fashioned. Are you sure the ship is smart?"

"I am. It's like in the old song. You know: 'Because, because, because, because…because of the wonderful things he does.'"

"Are you saying the ship does wonderful things?"

"Yup."

"Like what?"

"You'll see. In the meantime, you should download the ship's app onto your phone so you can follow along."

Ernie took out his phone and showed Flynn a diagram displaying the ship's current position above the Moon. In the representation there, the ship looked from the outside like a slowly spinning football, but more rounded, like a Rugby ball. Then he showed

Flynn how to download the app.

They walked on for a while. Finally, Ernie said, "Okay kid, now you tell me something."

"Sure. What?"

"Tell me about that sign you were staring at yesterday. What's the Omega Problem? And how do we solve it?"

"Ah. Well, it's a planet."

"What planet?"

"It's not one of the locals, so to speak. It's a rogue."

"Okay. Do you mean *rogue* like…it doesn't follow the rules?"

"Ha. Sort of," Flynn said. "It certainly doesn't follow the rule that says a planet's supposed to orbit a star. This one was ejected from its star system due to a nova, a close stellar encounter, or a galactic collision. Something like that."

"Can you just tell it like in *Astronomy for Dummies*?"

"Umm…okay. It's like those good news/bad news jokes. Bad news: there's an explosion or something in a distant star system. Good news: one planet doesn't get destroyed; it only gets thrown out. Bad news: now it's doomed to zip around the galaxy all by itself—cold, dark, and without a star to warm it."

"That I understand."

"Hmm. So, good news: for millions of years, it zips through the Milky Way and doesn't run into anything. But bad news: about ten years ago, we found out it was headed straight for us."

"For *us*?"

"Well, for our solar system anyway. The media made a big deal about how it was going to destroy civilization."

"Yeah, I remember that. Lots of news stories for a year."

"Yup. They named the rogue star Omega, for the last letter in the Greek alphabet."

"You mean like in, *I am the alpha and the omega?*"

"Uh…yes. So, are you a biblical scholar?"

"Nope. I just read it sometimes."

"Anyway, it was scary stuff for a while. But good news: it missed the solar system. Then bad news: Omega's passing had stirred up a whole lot of stuff out beyond Pluto, dwarf planets and such. Some of those went further out, but some of them fell inward and now a few of those are headed toward Earth."

"More bad news then?"

"Yes, but there's also good news: the largest dwarf, 23097 Galera, has already passed through Earth's orbit. It wasn't even close, so that was no problem, nor did it get much news coverage. We've analyzed the trajectories of the remaining Omega stuff and determined that none of them will hit the Earth."

"That's good. So, what's the bad news now?"

"Nothing that I know of. There's just this nagging feeling that we might have missed something."

"Like what?"

"That's the problem we have to solve. It's also part of the reason for this trip: to look around the outer planets and make sure there aren't any more surprises out there."

"I certainly hope not." Ernie's app beeped. He looked at it and said, "Speaking of bad news, we gotta get back to the bridge. There's trouble again."

"Again?"

"It's the shakedown part of our flight—you know, solving minor problems, working out the kinks. But don't worry. It's nothing out of the ordinary."

"Nothing out of the ordinary," however, turned out to be a man pointing a gun at the captain. "Stay back or I'll shoot!" he hollered as Flynn and Ernie approached.

"Whatever you say," Ernie replied.

The captain said, "How can we help you, sir?"

"I'm taking over the ship!"

"That's not possible," said the captain. He was standing straight and tall and looking every bit a man in command of the situation.

Flynn wondered, *What is the captain doing out here in the middle of the night, and in dress uniform?*

"You think it's not possible?" asked the gunman. "Just watch me!"

"I am watching," said the captain, "and I see you have a gun."

"So?"

"Guns are not allowed aboard this ship."

"Really?"

"We search the luggage thoroughly to prevent them from coming aboard."

"Then I guess you didn't search mine thoroughly enough."

"Apparently so."

"So now, I have the only gun on this ship."

"Also apparent."

"And that means I'm in total control! Captain, you will now turn over the command of this ship to me. Remove all your men from the bridge. You will remain as my hostage."

"I'm afraid I can't allow that."

"Don't make me shoot you."

"That would be unpleasant. But I must urge you, for your own safety, not to fire that weapon."

"And that's your final answer?"

"It is."

"Then a demonstration is necessary!" The gunman swung

around and aimed at Ernie's chest.

"No, wait!" yelled Flynn.

He moved toward Ernie, tripped and fell, his arms outflung. He saw the flash of the gun. He felt the bullet in his chest. He dropped down into darkness.

•••

The captain looked down at Flynn's body. "Who's the kid, Ernie?"

"His name is Hopper, sir."

"The troublemaker?"

"I don't think so. He's just young…and a little dumb."

"And brave. Is he hurt?"

"I think he fainted, is all."

"Good. Why don't you sign him onto the crew."

"I'd be happy to, sir. One two-hundredth?"

"Make it one one-fiftieth. For trying to save a valued member of my crew."

"Thank you, sir. I will."

"He gets the bullet too. We've both got enough already."

"Yes sir. It'll make a good souvenir."

"Fine. Carry on." The captain turned toward the bridge. Then he turned back. "Oh, and Ernie, one more thing…"

•••

"Wake up, kid!" Ernie lifted Flynn up and shook him a little.

Flynn said, "What…" and reached for his chest.

"There's no blood, kid. Just a bruise. It's probably tender so…"

"Ouch!"

"Told ya. Here, drink this."

"Is it alcoholic?"

"Very. It's from the captain's stock, so it's good stuff. You earned it."

The stuff, whatever it was, went down burning but…oh…yeah.

"What happened?" Flynn asked when he could speak again.

"You got shot."

"I knew that part already. What I mean is, umm, why am I not dead?"

"I told you. Guns are very dangerous. They're not allowed onboard."

"So then how did I get shot by what—I will swear in court—was a gun?"

"All right, fine, kid. But this is going to sound a little weird."

"Weirder than it already is?"

"Maybe. You see, it isn't any of us, the crew, who doesn't allow guns."

"Who then?"

"The ship."

"The ship doesn't allow guns?"

"No, it doesn't. So, when somebody shoots a gun, the ship makes sure it won't happen again. We tried to warn the guy. We always warn 'em, but they never listen. See, this same thing happens almost every trip, and right about here too. You know, in lunar orbit, on the first night. That's why the captain wears his dress uniform for the first night. The bullet-proof vest fits better inside it. You didn't have a vest, so that's why you got hurt. The bullet wasn't going fast enough to penetrate, but it was going fast enough to sting. See?" Ernie held up a small, bright, coppery thing. "Okay?"

"Slow down, Ernie, and back it up a bit. Exactly how does the ship make sure it won't happen again?"

"Ah." Ernie sat down next to Flynn, with his back against the wall. "Well," he said, "the ship is very good at tunneling."

"You told me that already too."

"So, when somebody shoots a gun, a tunnel just happens to open up behind them. Or two tunnels. More like a tunnel within a tunnel, but with different lengths, so there's a differential…uh… we don't know how it works."

"Just say it like in *Spaceships for Dummies*."

"Okay. The gun fires, the bullet goes one way, and the gun goes the other way, only in this case the gun ends up moving farther than the bullet."

"Then the gunman, who was holding this gun, goes with it?"

"Yeah."

"And now he's out there somewhere?"

"In lunar orbit, yes. All safe and sound and not going to kill anybody. I told you; the ship does wonderful things."

"Uh huh. Can I have another swallow of that stuff?"

"Sure thing, kid. We can both use a little, so I'll join you."

●

CHAPTER 3

THE PRISONER'S DILEMMA

Flynn sat in the mess hall, drinking coffee, thinking of ways to say what needed to be said. He decided to try the simple approach.

He texted: *Hi. I don't know if you heard, but I got shot. I'm OK though.*

Ernie asked, "Is that your girlfriend?"

"More than that. She's my fiancée, Louise."

"Ah."

Louise sent: *What? You got shot? How? Are you OK? Do you need a doctor?*

Flynn: *I'm fine. It's just an ugly bruise. No doctor needed.*

"Is she taking it well?"

"I'm not sure. Ernie, you've been shot a couple of times. What do you tell your…girlfriend? Wife?"

"Ex-wife. I usually tell her I'm not dead. Then she says, 'Better luck next time.'"

"I'm sorry to hear that."

"Don't be."

Louise sent, *I want video. Or a picture. Now!*

Flynn replied, *Hold on a sec.*

"Ernie, can you take my picture?"

"Sure. Hand it over."

"Let me get my shirt off."

"All right." Ernie looked around the mess hall. It was sparse, but not empty. "Nobody here will misunderstand me taking a naked picture of you, will they?"

"I'm not naked. Just topless."

"At least put on a smile."

Ernie took the photo. Flynn sent it.

She sent back, *You're right that is ugly! And the bruise looks bad too.*

Flynn sent a smiley face, because he was smiling. He said, "Ernie, can you leave us alone? We've got some mushy stuff to send."

"Sure kid. Sometimes I wish I was young again, but then I come to my senses."

●●●

The starship *De Profundis* fell outward and down, and in the first hour of the first watch it began falling toward Mars. There were screens around the ship showing a view of the red planet. From time to time the view shifted as the Day Pro worked on getting comfortable in its new orbit. Finally, it settled in with a sigh. Or at least, the crew sighed. It was time to begin the work of transferring people and cargo from the ship to the various bases below. It would be at least a week before the ship started its journey to the outer planets.

Ernie now left Flynn alone during the first watch, though he still showed up from time to time, taught Flynn more about being part of the Bosun's crew, and turned over more responsibilities. Flynn was still a part of the scientific community too, so he got to attend some of the conferences aboard. He was especially interested in conferences on the Omega Problem. He had sent his notes on it to Professor Lonigan, but so far Lonigan had been too busy to reply. There were also conferences on the Martian surface, but he was only allowed to attend those remotely. So, he sat in front of other scientists and learned, and he walked with Ernie and learned. It was good to learn.

Unfortunately, after a week, Flynn got bored. This is how the trouble started:

Flynn: "I wish I could go down there."

Ernie: "Where?"

Flynn: "To the Martian surface, of course. I can see it on the screens, but I can't touch it. This is a once-in-a-lifetime opportunity and I'm going to miss it."

Ernie: "So? Put in for shore leave."

Flynn: "Really? How?"

Ernie: "It's simple. Use the app. I'll approve it."

The Day Pro app was easy and instructive on this point, but disappointing. The Russian base only accepted Russians. The American base accepted everyone, but all the slots were full. The

Chinese base, on the other hand, only had one slot open…

…and the Chinese base was also well-designed and, for a Martian outpost, expansive. The corridors were clean, the lighting was bright, and everyone seemed intent on accomplishing some task somewhere in another part of the base. There was, however, a concession stand that rented spacesuits and golf carts for outside excursions. It was expensive, but as Flynn had said, it was also a once-in-a-lifetime chance. He drove out to the end of the track, then walked further onto a small ridge. For a long time, he sat there, watching small dust devils in the valley and the way the distant sun glowed through the atmospheric haze. He stayed until his oxygen alarm went off, then hurried back. The concession operator seemed annoyed that he had been out so long.

He strolled along the corridor leading back to the base's center. An attractive woman passed, going the other direction. Flynn stopped, turned, and called out tentatively, "Cassandra?"

She seemed to freeze in her tracks. Slowly she turned. "Flynn!"

They hugged. It seemed to Flynn that she had been sad but welcomed this chance to think about something else. He stepped back. There were tears in her eyes.

"I'm sorry if I upset you," he said.

"Oh, it's not you. It's just been so long since I heard my English name." She smiled. "But it's good to hear it. From you." They hugged again.

Three years back, Flynn had sat next her at a conference in Boise. They started talking during a break, then whispering through the lecture. They ate lunch together, and dinner, and lunch, and dinner again. There had been hugs before parting at the airport. For a while they had corresponded regularly. She got married. He got engaged.

She took his hand. "Why don't we go to my quarters and talk," she said.

He said, "Okay."

Her quarters were small but well-furnished. They sat down. She asked about Louise. He told her the good news and added, "How's Richard?"

"He's very excited these days. He's been working on the Omega Problem for a year, and now—he's up there aboard your ship. He'll be going along with you to the outer planets."

"That's great. It's too bad you can't come too."

"I'm not allowed."

"What?"

"Couples are not permitted to travel together. There's too much chance of defection, especially since Richard is English."

"You're kidding…about defection I mean."

"No, I'm not. That's why they recruited us for Mars. We're both scientists, and since we're married, they have more leverage to keep us here."

"Oh, wow. I didn't know. So, if Richard is up there (he pointed), is it okay if I'm here in your quarters?"

"Don't worry," she said. "I'm sure we're well chaperoned."

"How's that?"

"There are monitors here. I'm not sure exactly where, since they do great things with miniaturization these days. But I'm certain they're watching us right now."

"Why?"

"We met in the hallway. You're foreign. I'm Chinese. What more reason is there?"

"Are they listening too?"

"Of course."

"Wow. I've never been under surveillance before."

"That you know about."

"True. And guess what: I'm a bit nervous. It's like suddenly finding yourself on one of those reality TV shows. I don't know what to do with my hands."

"Just keep them to yourself and everything will be fine."

He laughed. She laughed. Everything was fine.

They had tea. She cooked dinner. He helped clean up. They hugged once more at the door. He whispered briefly in her ear, then said aloud, "I'm sorry I forgot your birthday."

She said, "It doesn't matter. Besides, that was two months ago."

"Yes, but I still feel bad about it. Tell you what: the ship leaves tonight, but I'll try to get you something before then. I'll send it down."

"Thanks, but you don't have to."

"I want to."

"Okay. Thank you." They hugged again. He left. She watched him walk away, then closed the door.

●●●

The base security room was quiet that night, except for a group gathered around one monitor. They were pointing and laughing. Since laughter and security were seldom heard together, Supervisor Chang felt the need to intervene. The conversation that followed was in Chinese, but it went something like this:

Supervisor: What is going on here?

Subordinate 1: We're watching Subject Koh.

Supervisor: And why is that?

Subordinate 1: She received a package from the ship.

Supervisor: I assume you checked it thoroughly.

Subordinate 1: Very thoroughly, Supervisor. It contained a cake.

Supervisor: Did you scan it?

Subordinate 1: No. We ate it.

Supervisor: That was foolish. There might have been poison.

Subordinate 1: There was no poison, Supervisor. Just a capitalist overload of sugar. It was disgusting.

Subordinate 2: Very disgusting.

Subordinate 3: Almost unpalatable.

Supervisor: Is there any of this suspicious cake remaining?

Subordinate 1: No, Supervisor. We delivered the package to her. But—we left enough crumbs so that she would know what it was.

Subordinate 3: Now we're watching her cry. She's beautiful. I would like to go and comfort her.

Supervisor: Suspect interrogations are my responsibility. I will attend to it later.

Subordinate 1: She's getting a text message!

Supervisor: What does it say?

Subordinate 1: It's in English.

Supervisor: Run it through the translator.

They all peered at the screen. Some of the words, being uncommon, could not be translated. The original message was:

I'm sorry you can't make it. I know it's hard news to take, but at least it's not a black mark on your career. Please cheer up. You know, in Treasure Island, Long John Silver received a black mark. It was meant for death, but Long John turned it around and used it for life. I hope you will do the same.

Supervisor: This is obviously nonsense.

Subordinate 2: You are right as always, Supervisor.

Subordinate 3: She's taking the wrapping paper out of her

waste bin and... she's holding it up to the light. Now she's going into the bedroom.

Supervisor: It's a secret message! Send guards immediately!

An alarm was sent. They all peered at the screen. For a while, nothing happened. Then the soldiers burst into the apartment. They looked around briefly, then crashed through the bedroom door. The angle of the monitor was bad, but through the ruined door they caught a glimpse of Subject Koh's head seeming to disappear into the floor. Then the soldiers rushed forward and stabbed with their bayonets...into a piece of brown wrapping paper, blank except for one, carefully drawn, black circle.

CHAPTER 4

ORGANIZED LABOR

The ship departed the Martian orbit a little behind schedule, due to a party the Day Pro scientists threw for the Martian scientists remaining behind. Apparently, the ship's supply of Earth-distilled booze was hard to say goodbye to, so the actual departure occurred in the second watch.

At the time, Flynn was asleep, dreaming of the planets. They were all laid out in order from innermost to outermost, and *De Profundis* was sailing along a smooth curve that touched them all. He said, "No!" and opened his eyes.

He knew, of course, that the planets seldom aligned in the way they appeared in his dream. He realized, *On the other hand, for a ship that can fall to any point it chooses, the alignment doesn't matter.* He mumbled, "Yup," and rolled over to sleep some more, satisfied that his conscious mind had done its duty in correcting his unconscious mind. He didn't know if his unconscious was satisfied with its rebuttal, but he felt like it was.

A message from Bosun Schwarz beeped. The text read, "Come to my office."

Ernie asked, "How was your visit to the Chinese base?"

"Umm…very interesting and educational."

"Uh huh. Did you also happen to kidnap somebody while you were there?"

"No. Why?"

"The Chinese claim you did."

"Well, I did invite an old friend to tour the ship if she had the chance. Maybe she just forgot to go back."

"Possibly. But the captain interviewed the couple in question, and they said something different. "

"What?"

"That she was a virtual prisoner there, that you rescued her, and that they're both extremely grateful."

"Oh…that kidnapping. So, am I in trouble?"

"Well, it's up to the Review Board to make the final decision."

"Who's on the Review Board?"

"It's just me."

"And has the Board decided anything yet?"

"No. But tell me: why'd you do it, really?"

"I don't know…I think maybe I fell in love with her the first time I met her. I guess I still am."

"I thought you were in love with Louise?"

"I am."

"But you're fooling around with this other woman?"

"No, I'm not fooling around."

"I meant sex."

"So did I. You know, my undergrad school once invited a popular professor to give us a lecture on sex."

"Well, that's one way to fill a lecture hall. What did he say?"

"He told us the tragic tale of Amnon and Tamar."

"Old Testament?"

"Yes. And then he said, 'Love is when you want what's best for the other person.'"

"Oh. I hadn't thought of it that way. Good point, though."

"Yeah. And that's why I did it. I just want her to be happy."

"Okay. I'm sure the Review Board will take your…umm, explanation…into account."

"Thanks. So, can I go now?"

"Nope. One more thing."

"What's that?

"I understand you also drove a golf cart out on the Martian surface."

"Yes. Why?"

"A golf cart? Really? You gotta be kiddin' me."

"What did you expect? A high-tech something from NASA?"

"Well…yeah."

"Actually, I asked the concessionaire about that. He said they originally stole some plans from NASA. They were easy to steal but expensive to make. So then they stole some plans from Club Car. They were hard to steal, but relatively cheap to make. And they worked just as well, so…"

"Okay, never mind. That's not the important part."

"What then?"

"Did you wear a spacesuit while you were out tooling around on that cart?"

"Yes."

"For how long?"

"Two or three hours, I guess."

"Good. That makes you qualified."

"For what?"

"We need to make an unplanned, dirt-side excursion in the asteroid belt."

"Why?"

"Because we've got labor troubles there."

•••

Flynn and Ernie slid down onto the asteroid's surface. Ernie bounced, pirouetted back to watch Flynn, and nailed his landing. Flynn sprawled, rolled, and crashed. Ernie helped him up. "Be careful," he radioed. "These suits are expensive."

"And heavy," replied Flynn. "High inertia and low gravity take some getting used to."

"Then let me show you." Ernie bounced away. Flynn watched his technique, then tried it himself. His effort was passible.

"What is this place?" Flynn asked.

"Croesus. It's a metal-rich asteroid."

"You've been here before, haven't you?"

"Yeah, I spent a lot of time here. Captain Wagner and I, and some other guys, we started a mine here. It was the first ever on an asteroid."

"Successful?"

"Not at first. Sure, we pulled out some valuable ore, but our expenses were extremely high. Plus, there was a lot of risk. There were accidents and injuries. We were about to give up the whole thing and go home."

"What happened?"

"We lost a guy. We held his funeral service on the surface. At the end, we were all looking up at the stars, when suddenly this huge rock winked into existence right over our heads. So, we took a shuttle over and tried to land on it, but somehow we fell into it instead. That was scary. I thought maybe we'd be trapped inside and die there. It was dark, but as we wandered around a few lights came on. We finally got to the command center, with all its equipment running, but still not a soul around. I said to the captain, 'This is really creepy.' He agreed. Then I said, 'I wish we were back at Earth'. A moment later, we were."

"Were what?"

"Back at Earth, or at least in Earth orbit. That's when we realized that it was a spaceship, and that we'd stumbled into a treasure. We checked around for owners, but didn't find any, so we claimed salvage rights. That's when we got out of the mining business and into the transportation business. Less risk and more profit."

"But your asteroid mine is still active?"

"We found some workers who like the environment."

"Who's that?"

"Well, if I know these guys, they're out there now, watching us." Ernie scanned with a handheld light.

Flynn looked around. The sky was dark but glittering with a million stars. The asteroid's horizon was marked by huge boulders that blocked a few of those stars. It was also very close. As Ernie's beam passed over the ground, Flynn noticed that the dust was marked everywhere with footprints and tracks. Then he saw a face peering around a rock. At least, it was in the shape of a face, but there were no discernable features like eyes or mouths. Ernie kept his light pointed at the thing. Slowly, it rose up and turned away, moving on lots of legs. Ernie swung around and caught another thing, only this one moved on wheels. Flynn sensed there were more of them, all around in the darkness.

"Are those robots?"

"Yup. They were on the Day Pro when we found it, down in what we call the Lower Depths, which is really the outer part of the ship. They were doing maintenance."

"Are there a lot of them?"

"Yup. We figure they're a whole colony."

"How do you mean?"

"You know, they're a society, or a tribe, or whatever. They've got a hierarchy, laws, culture – all that stuff. They've got old ones, young ones, and even baby ones."

"How do robots have babies?"

"The same way we do. They make 'em."

Flynn and Ernie entered a tunnel, then an airlock. They got out of the spacesuits. They opened the inner door and passed into a hallway. Flynn still found walking difficult. "Why didn't we just tunnel in here and skip the surface?" he asked.

"For safety," Ernie explained. "The office might have sprung a leak, depressurized, or collapsed. I told you; this place is very dangerous. Enough bad things happened when we were here before that I get nervous if there isn't a spacesuit nearby."

"So how did you convince the robots to take it over?"

"We didn't. They convinced us."

"They *wanted* to work here?"

"They wanted a place of their own, and working here was a way to get it. We helped them set up an independent colony, where they could do their own thing. They mine the ore and process it right here. We buy their products and re-sell them for a nice profit. We hire some of them to work on the ship's maintenance. We sell them equipment and parts. They sell us repair services, and so on. It's all worked well, until now."

"What now?"

"You'll see. Here's the office."

The office contained desks, chairs, lamps, a seven-foot-tall humanoid robot, a couple of filing cabinets, and a calendar on the wall. Flynn took a seat at Ernie's gesture. Ernie sat down behind a desk. He said, "Hello Cyrus."

The robot said, "Hello Ernie. Welcome back."

"It's good to be back," Ernie lied.

"We're glad to have you here," the robot said. Flynn couldn't tell if this was the truth. He guessed that having no face would be helpful for playing poker. The robot advanced into the room and squatted so that his…where his eyes should be…was at Flynn's level. It added, in a pleasant voice, "And who is this?"

Ernie answered, "Flynn Hopper, bosun's crew."

"Nice to meet you, Mr. Hopper." The robot held out its hand. Flynn felt a moment of panic. Was he supposed to shake hands? Would all his bones be pulverized? "You might want this," it added. Flynn looked down. There was a headset in the robot's hand. Flynn took it.

"Don't put it on," Ernie cautioned. "It's just a bunch of noise."

Flynn looked at the robot. "Thank you," he said.

The robot called Cyrus turned to Ernie. "I would offer you something to eat and drink," it said, "but there was an accident. The food storage facilities went offline."

"We're not planning on staying that long anyway."

"Then let's get down to business, as you say. Are you paying with cash, check, or services?"

"How much?"

"100 million."

"That's outrageous! We couldn't even sell the whole lot for that much."

"Nevertheless, that's our price."

Flynn put on the headset. Ernie was right: it was mostly noise, but it was better than listening to those two argue. He looked around. The calendar, which was several years out of date, was a type called "pinup." It featured a model named Roxy Sinclair on the February page. Flynn stood up and wandered over to check the other months. Roxy looked pretty good in all of them. Then he thought that, since the calendar had obviously been abandoned there, maybe nobody would mind if he borrowed it…

"What do you think, Flynn?"

He turned around to see that Ernie was looking at him. "The robots won't go for it at any price," he replied and thought, *Why did I say that?*

"Why do you say that?" Ernie asked.

"Umm, because their congress has voted against every bid you've made so far."

"That's crazy. The robots don't even have a congress."

"Actually, we do," said Cyrus, "and Mr. Hopper is right. They've vetoed all your offers." His non-face was turned toward Flynn. Flynn wished desperately for eyes there.

"Who told you?" demanded Ernie. "Do you hear voices in that headset?"

"Umm, no. It's noise like you said, but…there are patterns too. It rises and falls, plus there are tones and pitches. It's almost like an orchestra: woodwinds, strings, brass, and drums."

"So, you've got a band in there? What are they playing?"

"Nothing I recognize."

"I give up. I can't talk any sense into Mr. Negative Electrode here. And you're no help either, Flynn, so…you take over."

"Me? Okay. All right. Umm, Mr. Cyrus?"

"Just Cyrus."

"Ok. Cyrus, we know that money isn't the issue."

"What makes you think that?"

"I just think it. There *is* an issue but…I'm not sure what it is. In any case your congress is anxious for you to make a deal."

"How can you say there's an issue if you don't know what it is?"

"Oh, it's there all right. So why don't you just make your counteroffer?"

"Who said I had one?"

"You wanted me to have this headset, so don't complain if I use it."

"Fine, then. I would like to go with you to the outer planets."

"You mean, you want to come along on the Day Pro's expedition?"

"Yes."

"Okay. So, what will you give us in return, if we let you join us?"

"That depends on whether you let me bring some others of our colony."

Flynn had another thought. "You don't want 'some' others, do you? You want to bring them all, right?"

"Yes."

"Why?"

"We've been on this asteroid a long time. It's good, but we're really a space-faring tribe. We need to get back into practice. Plus, we have young ones who've never been on a spaceship. We'd like to teach them."

"And if we say yes to all of that?"

"Then the cargo is yours, free of charge."

"Wait a minute!" Ernie interjected. "You can't just pick up, leave, and shut down the mine!"

"But we can. And we have. As of this moment, we're on strike."

"We won't stand for that!" yelled Ernie. "We'll lock you out!"

"How will you do that," asked Cyrus, "since our colony is inside the mine, while your ship is outside?"

Flynn held up his hand. "Wait a minute, Ernie. Cyrus has one more detail to add."

The faceless face turned to Flynn again, stayed there for a long moment, and then said, "Yes. We will also offer to resume mining here on this asteroid once the Day Pro returns."

"That's it?" Ernie asked.

"That's it."

"And the cargo is free if we agree to those terms?"

"Only this cargo. Any future cargoes will be at the standard price."

"All right," said Ernie. "Let me check with the captain." He got up and went to a corner of the office to make his call.

Flynn held out the headset to Cyrus. "Thank you. I'll give this back to you."

"No need, Mr. Hopper. The set is complimentary. Please, take it with you."

"Thanks. Umm, can I take something else?"

•••

Flynn and Ernie went into the airlock to put on their spacesuits.

Flynn asked, "Can't we just tunnel back from here?"

Ernie held up a black circle. "I'm already ahead of you kid. But put on the spacesuit first. Those things don't grow on trees."

Flynn said, "We're okay then…I guess."

Ernie asked, "What's wrong? Dealing with the robots' hive mind? None of us knew about *that* before. Good thing you figured it out."

"It's not really a hive mind, not all the time anyway. They're individuals, but they can connect their minds together when they want to. That's their 'congress.'"

"So, what is it you're worried about?"

"Cyrus didn't tell us everything."

"What else is new?"

"That orchestra I thought I heard. Sometimes the woodwinds, the brass, and the strings would come in. Sometimes they contended with each other, and then faded out again. But the drums, they kept a steady beat in the background the whole time."

"Meaning what?"

"Meaning it was like a chant, as though they were repeating 'fix it, fix it.'"

"Fix what? The Omega Problem you told me about?"

"Maybe."

"Ok. So how would abandoning the mine fix that?"

"I don't know. But they're afraid of something here."

CHAPTER 5

WHEN YOU WISH UPON A STAR...

Flynn sat in the mess hall, eating his dinner. Professor Parks set her breakfast down opposite him. She was bright, cheery, well-groomed and well-dressed, as always. Flynn thought she might be attractive, even if she was in her mid-thirties.

She said, "Good morning!"

"Huh?" he replied. "Oh, yes, I guess it is morning."

"What's wrong, Flynn? You don't look well."

"It's nothing."

"Don't say that. What is it? Bad news from home?"

"Home is a long way away now."

"I know! Four point two astronomical units! Isn't it great?"

"No, it's not."

"Oh," she said, "I see. You're homesick. You miss your girlfriend, don't you?"

"Louise. Fiancée. She sent me a text."

"Bad news? Dear John?"

"No, nothing like that. Good news, I guess."

"But you miss her terribly, now, don't you?"

"Yes."

"Have you ever been to Antarctica, Flynn?"

"What?"

"Scientific station. Bottom of the world. Ice. Snow. You know?"

"Oh. Yeah. No."

"Didn't think so. I have. Why don't you come to the party tonight and I'll tell you all about it."

"Party?"

"The scientists are throwing a party to celebrate our arrival at Jupiter."

"Oh? I didn't know."

"I'm sorry you weren't invited. But I'll make it up to you."

"How?"

"You'll be my date tonight."

"I don't know. If they didn't want me in the first place, then maybe I shouldn't…"

"They didn't not want you. They just didn't think about you."

"They didn't?"

"They're too wrapped up in themselves, all excited about being the first humans out here, true explorers that they are. Plus, they're swimming in data about the planets and the Sun, enough to write papers for years—for their whole careers, in fact. They're in hog heaven."

"Will there be alcohol?"

"Yes. Good food too."

"Okay, I'm in."

"Terrific. Meet me here at seven."

"Uh…"

"Nineteen hundred hours, sailor."

"Yes, ma'am."

"Now you're making me feel old."

"I'm sorry. You don't look old…uh…I mean…"

"Stop digging that hole, Flynn."

"Okay. By the way, have you seen it?"

"Seen what?"

"Jupiter."

"Of course I have. It's been on the screens all day."

"I mean, have you seen it yourself? With your own eyes?"

"Oh. No."

"Would you like to?"

He took her past the bridge, down a hallway, and up a flight of stairs to a small landing. There he caught her arm. "Be careful. The gravity's less up here." Then he produced a set of keys and unlocked a small door. He fumbled inside, found a switch, and turned it on. They walked down another passage, glad that they could hold onto the walls. Then there was a spiral staircase. They crawled up it, on hands and knees, into a circular chamber topped with a clear dome. And there it was.

"It's best to sit down with your back against the wall."

"Okay. Wow."

They couldn't see the end of it in any direction. It was all there, everywhere: the colors, the complex patterns, the violence so close at hand. And way up, above the clouds—"down and beneath," she corrected him—they caught glimpses of a strong blue glow, the burning heart of that vast engine.

"It's scary," she said, "and fascinating too. I could stay here all day."

"Best not to, though, because of…"

"The radiation. I know. All right, show me the way back. After all, you've got fresh sperm to protect."

"What?"

"Fresh sperm. They're produced in your testicles and mixed with semen during e—are you blushing, Flynn?"

"No. The radiation is getting to me. That's all."

"If you say so. Too bad, though. It's secluded here. Wouldn't it be fun to make love in this chamber, with the great view and less than one percent gravity? Okay, okay, I'm right behind you. Wait up!"

They returned to the mess hall. "Thanks for the tour," she said. "I loved it."

"You're welcome."

"By the way," she added, "wear some nice civvies tonight, not this old coverall…which seriously needs washing. You know where the laundry is. Pre-soak it. And take a shower too."

"Yes ma'am."

"See you tonight. then."

•••

Flynn found some good civvies in his duffel. They weren't great, but they were clean and not too bad looking. He hoped the wrinkles wouldn't show up in the ship's evening lighting.

Professor Parks, on the other hand, showed up in high heels

and a cocktail dress. He realized she could be gorgeous, especially when she put on makeup. "Is that eye shadow?" he asked.

"Yes," she said. "It's called 'The Amazon.' Why don't we find a table over there in the corner? Then you can get us drinks. I think red wine for me. There's steak on the menu tonight."

"Whatever 'steak' is on this ship."

"No, it really is steak, courtesy of Dr. Lonigan. He arranged for it just so we can celebrate this milestone."

"That's nice, I guess."

"Yes, maybe he has some problems, but he's really a sweetheart who can be quite generous at times."

"A steak would hit the spot right now, that's for sure. As long as..."

"Don't worry. I put your name in, so you're included in the count. Otherwise, you could have mine. I'm not too much into meat."

"Sorry to hear that. I'll go get the drinks."

Flynn stood in line at the bar, listening to the scientists excitedly discuss their discoveries, potential discoveries, and theories. Some of them argued competing ideas, but with good nature and humor. Good moods prevailed.

Dinner was delicious. The wine was nice. The professor was beautiful. Even though they were sitting in a corner, several men made their way over to say hi to her, discuss 'important' research they were thinking of doing, or to simply compliment her on the dress. Flynn found he was staring at it himself. He thought that might be impolite, so he tried to engage her in some sort of conversation. It didn't work. She watched him watching her but didn't offer to help him out. She just waited.

"Umm," he said at last, "you were going to tell me about

Antarctica."

"It's cold," she said.

Flynn laughed. "I thought I was bad at conversation, but you're rotten at it."

She laughed. "You're right. Sorry."

"'Cold' is a good start, though."

"Cold, yes," she said. "And isolated. You're in small, sterile, utilitarian quarters that aren't very appealing, without much to do except work, but you don't go outside because the environment can kill you."

"Kind of like where we are at the moment."

"Precisely. That's my point."

"Which is?"

"There's a special kind of loneliness you get there. It's a sort of desperation, and you feel an extra need for human contact."

"That makes sense."

"I'm talking about close human contact. Only you don't have any friends there, just colleagues, associates, and people you hardly know."

"That must be tough."

"So…you make arrangements." She looked at him.

"Oh sure. I get it. You need somebody to talk with, just chit-chat, meet for dinner, talk about old times and so on."

"I'm glad you understand," she said, looking disappointed.

So, they moved on to chitchat. They told each other about their childhoods, their families, their families' dysfunctions. It was a pleasant time.

After dinner the older scientists were gathered around a couple of tables on the other side of the mess hall. Their arguments were more animated now. Professor Parks looked over at them and remarked, "Lonigan thinks there's high probability that at least one of the Omega dwarfs will intersect the Sun."

"He does? That's good. I think so too."

"Is that what you put in the notes you sent him?"

"Yes. How did you know?"

"Lonigan used your notes in his formal presentation this morning."

"What makes you think they were mine?"

"The math was too good. Usually, Lonigan's needs help."

"Which you provide?"

"I do. I edit yours too. I can tell your style. Those were your notes, but your name wasn't mentioned in his talk."

"Oh. It wasn't? Not at all? Not even a citation?"

"Not a word."

"Crap."

"First time getting stolen, huh? That's always a shock to your system."

"Does Lonigan do it often?"

"No, not very. But sometimes he does. I think everybody either steals ideas or gets them stolen, sooner or later. So, get used to it."

"I'll try but it's depressing."

"It is." She stood up and held out her hand. "On that note, let's go someplace more cheerful."

She took him to her quarters, invited him in, and closed the door. "You know, we need to focus on being in Jupiter orbit for the first time."

"You mean, *Where no man has gone before?*"

"No *one*," she said, "and that's important. I think this situation calls for a top-down celebration."

"What's a top-down celebration?"

She didn't answer but turned away from him instead. "Unzip me," she said.

He did.

She turned back to him. "Now…pull my top down."

He thought: *A moment like this requires courage.* He reached out, put his fingers inside the dress, and pulled it down.

He stared. They were perfect. She asked, "So? What do you think?" He didn't want to talk but knew that words would be important, if only he could find some.

They came unbidden. "*Her breasts were like champagne glasses.*"

"What?"

"It's something I read in a book. Two prisoners are communicating by tapping on the walls. The long-time prisoner asks the new prisoner about his last liaison. The new guy taps back, 'Her breasts were like champagne glasses,' and that was all that he needed to say."

"Then that's all that you need to say. Thank you."

"You're welcome."

"Now go ahead and touch me."

He reached up, but she leaned forward and hugged him. He put his arms around her and stroked her bare back. "Is that perfume?" he asked.

"It's essential oil."

"Whatever it is, it's nice. It kind of reminds me…"

He was suddenly overwhelmed by her scent, the feel of her skin, and the warmth of her body. It was as though he'd grabbed an electrical wire and couldn't let go. He had no thoughts or volition, only the need to hold on. She stood still, listening to his breathing and the little sounds he made. Neither said anything.

After a long while he came back. He managed to say, "Sorry.

I don't know what happened there."

She murmured, "Neither do I. But don't be sorry. I enjoyed it."

"Really?"

"Yes. It was the best sex I've had in a long time, and I didn't even have to take my clothes off."

"So now what?"

She stepped back and looked at him. "So…it was tender, it was intimate, and I think we should just slip into bed and finish the job."

He said, "Umm…"

She asked, "Is there a problem?"

He said, "No. It's perfect. With that green eyeshadow, you're even my favorite fantasy."

"I am? Then I'm honored."

"And I'm ready. I can do this. I've got permission, so why not?"

She studied him carefully. She walked over to a dresser, took her necklace off, and looked in the mirror. "I appreciate your enthusiasm," she said. "But tell me—do you prefer top or bottom?"

He looked puzzled. "Top bunk? Top position?"

"Top," she repeated, "as in boss, versus bottom, as in minion. Or would you prefer to say 'dominant' and 'submissive?' I need to know."

"Why?"

"Because I'm the professor and you're the graduate assistant. That naturally makes me the top. Or would you like to switch? I'm easy, but you have to choose right now."

"I don't know…"

"Well, haven't you thought about it? Tell me, what do you do to us in those fantasies of yours?"

"*To us?*"

"I meant 'us,' as in green-skinned space vixens. We're quite popular in the literature."

"You are, and it's funny you should say that. I just got a message that made me think about you…all."

"I thought so, or something like that. I also don't think we should go to bed right now."

"You don't?"

"No. I've enjoyed our little time together, Flynn, but going to bed would ruin it. Let's leave it right there so I can cherish the memory."

"If you say so. I'm really sorry, Professor. Please don't be mad at me because I wouldn't…I mean I couldn't…"

"I won't. After all, it was probably better sex than anything else I'll get on this crate."

"I'm sorry."

"Just go, Flynn. Go now before I do something you'll regret."

He looked at her.

"No, it's all right," she said in a softer voice. "We can even do the old cliché."

"You mean like, let's still be friends?"

"Yes. Let's still be friends. Let's meet for breakfast every morning, just so we can talk. It'll be our little club."

"When you're having breakfast, I'm just getting off watch and eating dinner."

"Then we'll call it the Dinner Club."

"That sounds good."

"But Flynn, I warn you: I'm still going to wear this dress occasionally."

"When you do, I won't bother you."

"Oh no. Whenever I wear this dress, I *want* you to come talk to me. I want you to stare down the front of it, just the way you did at dinner tonight, and then walk away, because I want you to be terribly sad about what you're missing."

"I will," he said. "I promise."

•••

Flynn stood his watch. Not much was happening, so he had time to think about the message he'd gotten from Louise the previous morning.

She'd written, *I've been thinking about the green-skinned women. I know how it is on remote science stations, and I've decided that if it should happen, if you must, then I understand. It's alright. Just don't tell me about it. No, tell me about it. Just not a lot. You know what I mean.*

He decided it was time to answer. He wrote, *Funny you should say that. There really are green-skinned women here. I've even met one. But I'll tell you the truth: she was gorgeous and seductive and very willing. But, in the end, it wasn't meant to be. So that, I'm afraid, is the end of the story.*

He took a deep breath. He pressed the send icon. He knew that he wasn't connected directly to her phone, but the message would be queued into the ship's data stream. Since the text message didn't require much bandwidth and since it was still in the middle of the first watch, it would probably be sent almost instantaneously... except, of course, for the speed–of–light delay. At this distance from Earth, that would be around half an hour in each direction. Plus, she might not even be awake. He walked on and tried not to think about what she would say.

It was just over an hour later when he got her reply. *I'm sorry to hear that. Well, maybe I'm not. Yes, I AM sorry, because now you've only got one option and there's nothing we can do about it. Sorry.*

He thought briefly about Roxy Sinclair's February picture in his calendar. Then he thought about April and June. Then he thought about the art of pinup photography in general, and he muttered, 'Well, it might be worth a shot.'

His fingers trembled a little as he typed, *No. There's another option. Have you ever heard of sexting?* He hardly dared to breathe for the next hour, which made it difficult to walk his rounds.

She sent, *No. Tell me, how does sexting work?*

That was good. Very good. But now, how to put it delicately?

Another text came in. *Just kidding! I know exactly how it works. I hope you didn't take my joke seriously, did you?*

He furiously hit the backspace key on his reply.

Another text. *In fact, I've been wondering if I dared to send you some photos. I've got some good ones saved up. Now that I know you're interested, I'll pick the best one and send it. Just a sec.*

And then, *Done! It's queued up. I hope you like it. It's really naughty.* Larger files of a personal nature were assigned a much lower priority in the queue, behind scientific files and media coverage and texts. It was hard to tell how long the photo would take to arrive.

Another text. *But fair is fair. In return, please tell me all about what you're doing and thinking up there.*

Yes, he thought that might be fair.

Another text. *Did I just ask you to talk about feelings? Sorry! How about this - send me your first impression of my photo. No typing just hit the mic key, whisper something, and send. Then I'll whisper something else and send it back. I know there's a time delay but that just adds an element to it, don't you think?*

Yes, he thought, it certainly does.

Chapter 6

●

The Creeping Horror!

Flynn was called into a meeting in Captain Wagner's office. Ernie was there. So were Professors Lonigan, Parks, and Marcus. Lonigan frowned, Parks smiled, Marcus waived, and Captain Wagner said, "Sit down, Mr. Hopper."

"Yes sir. What's this about?"

"I think you know. Dr. Marcus tells me you're willing to volunteer for his proposed expedition down to the surface of Europa."

"Yes, sir. I'd be quite happy to."

"Plus," added Marcus, "he's already shown he's comfortable in a spacesuit environment. As a scientist, he knows how to correctly handle the collection of specimens."

As a scientist. Flynn glowed at the description. Now, they were going to include him. Plus, he would be the first man to walk on Europa, the fourth largest of Jupiter's moons, and currently the hottest prospect for other life, i.e., non-Earthly and non-Martian, in the solar system. He would be famous! He could finish his doctorate and be accepted to teach at any of the top universities! He would be—academically—a made man!

"This boy is one of our graduate assistants," said Dr. Lonigan, "and I don't want to risk him."

"But I've laid out a five-point protocol for safety," argued Dr. Marcus.

"It's not enough!" said Lonigan. They continued in that way for a while. Ernie raised his arms in a *can't help you* gesture. Dr. Parks reached out and squeezed his hand.

Finally, Lonigan turned to the captain. "Sir, I'm concerned about the safety of your ship," he said.

"In what way?"

"Dr. Marcus is right: there are probably aliens down there. But you don't want anything from down there accidently getting loose on the ship, in spite of his five-point protocol."

"Now wait a minute!" Dr. Marcus started to interject.

"No." Lonigan cut him off. "I'm not talking about something large with tentacles and teeth. A simple little microbe could wipe everybody out."

"Is that true?" Captain Wagner looked at Marcus.

"Theoretically…yes. But…"

"Then there won't be any expedition down to Europa. At least, not until we come up with better safety measures."

"Thank you, Captain."

The scientists filed out. Wagner asked Ernie and Flynn to stay.

"What do you think?" he asked.

"Scientists," said Ernie, as though that settled the matter.

"They're right," said Flynn. "But I really wanted to go. I would have been careful."

"I know that, Mr. Hopper. I appreciate your pioneering spirit, and I hope we can channel it into other areas."

"Sir?"

"What I'm trying to say is, I've got another job for you here on the ship, one that takes advantage of your natural inclination to explore."

"What's that, sir?"

"Well, you see, we don't have a complete map of the ship. There are tunnels running all through the hull. We've explored all the major ones, of course, but we still don't have the complete picture. I'd like you to fill it in for us."

"Yes, sir."

• • •

Flynn stood at the end of the tunnel. It terminated in a narrow shaft that went down into the hull outside the living area. He knelt on the lip of the shaft and aimed his flashlight down there. He could see smaller tunnels, round, and barely two feet across. They reminded him of "snake holes" in the bank of a stream. At least, that's what he and the other kids had called them back on the farm.

He didn't like these snake holes. First, they were creepy. Second, and maybe more importantly, they went through the narrowest part of the hull, which was also the part that endured the most stress. A single failure there would be almost immediately catastrophic.

It was important to check them out and make sure they weren't weakening the structure.

He sat back, switched off the light, and stared into the darkness. He listened for any sound, like creaking in the hull, hissing in the tunnels, or the sibilance of scaly bodies sliding by. Nothing. At last, he sighed, switched on the light, and chided himself for hesitation. He went over the edge, down into the shaft, picked a tunnel, and crawled headfirst into it, arms and flashlight extended.

It was a long tunnel. He had a lot to think about, including the fact that snakes didn't make snake holes. They didn't have the limbs and claws to do it. So, what could've made this? He stopped, switched off the light, and rested. He thought maybe he'd gone fifty yards. He switched on the light. There was nothing but more tunnel ahead. But what if…the tunnel caved in? A lot of rock loomed above him, pressing down. What held it up? How well could rock hold its own weight, especially with the extra stress of rotation? Maybe it wouldn't cave in but blow out instead, sending him off into space. Maybe it would be better to be crushed before being ejected into space.

Was that a chittering sound he heard up ahead? He listened carefully. Nothing.

What if…this was a sewer line? Would there be a sudden flush of rancid fluid, building up in the obstruction he formed, choking him and slowly filling up his lungs? What if it were a fuel line, or poisonous gas venting? Or a blast of fire? He switched off the light. He stilled his breathing, or tried to, and listened. Nothing.

What if…the tunnel narrowed? Would he get stuck? What if there were a grating somewhere up ahead, against which he would be trapped? He switched on the light. Nothing.

He decided…this wasn't a good idea. He decided…to get

out. But he couldn't turn around. No problem. He'd just crawl backwards. He scrabbled his feet and tried to get some purchase with his hands. He moved an inch. That was all. HE COULDN'T GO BACK!

How dumb could he be? Why did he do this?

He yelled. Could anybody hear him? Maybe, but would they know where he was? No. He was inside the walls in an unmapped tunnel. Nobody would find him. Nobody. Ever. NEVER. He was going to die right there!

Was he screaming? No, but he was making noise. Whimpering, crying…he wasn't sure. To die like this—it was horrible. Horrible. He yelled, "Help me! Help me!" over and over again.

And then the spider came.

It was there suddenly, chittering and clacking. It was so large that it nearly filled the tunnel. He tried to push it away with his hands. It didn't back up. He flailed at it. He yelled. Suddenly it rushed forward, stabbing and beating with its claws and legs. It bit into his arm and began twisting him over and over. His arms were wrapped in a web. No! *No!*

It began dragging him further into the tunnel. He tried to brace his legs, expand his chest, anything to stop from being pulled into that foul den. But the spider was so strong! Nothing worked! Nothing could halt it.

Now he screamed. And screamed again. And again. And he kept screaming until he was pulled into the nest, where he fell and lay on the floor, bruised, crying, and afraid.

Something very large approached and hovered over him. It made a noise, but he couldn't tell what the sound was, so filled were his ears with his own terror.

Flynn tried to control his breathing and to focus his eyes. Slowly, his vision cleared. The thing standing over him was seven feet tall, it was humanoid in shape, and it had no face.

It was Cyrus. The robot leaned down and put its faceless face next to his. It said, "What the hell do you think you're doing, Mr. Hopper?"

•••

Flynn said, "Wha...?"

Cyrus said, "What...the hell...were you...doing? Do you understand me now?"

Flynn said, "Yes. Umm, did you just curse? I didn't know robots could curse."

"We speak many languages, but in every situation, we use the appropriate one. So let me ask again..."

"I was exploring."

"On your own?"

"Yes. I mean, Captain Wagner asked me to. He wanted a map of the tunnels."

"Do you realize you caused severe panic among our robot spiders? They came pouring out of that tunnel, chattering about a creeping horror. I almost called for the Exterminator, but then I heard you yelling. Fortunately, I was able to get a volunteer to go in and get you out. She was very brave."

"I'm sorry about your spiders, I am, but frankly they scare the crap out of me."

Cyrus seemed to test the air. He said, "Yes. Literally."

"Why do you need spiders, anyway?"

"Because none of us can do what they do."

"What's that?"

"Repair the hull."

"The hull is solid rock."

"Tell me, over time, what happens to solid rock on earth?"

"Okay, I've got it. But why spiders?"

"Their body forms are some of the most prevalent and adaptable in the galaxy. You even have them on earth."

"That's what scares me."

"You weren't injured—fortunately—but trust me, you don't want to scare a spider."

"Why not?"

"Because our spiders can vomit molten rock at two thousand degrees when frightened. If that had happened in the tunnel here, you'd have died a horrible death. Plus, it would have taken extra time and resources to clean out your remains."

"That's comforting." Flynn held his arms up. "They also spin a very strong web. Can you get this off me?"

Cyrus said, "That web is ten times stronger than steel. Please don't struggle. A single strand of it could cut you in half."

"Will you get it off?"

"Yes, but not now. First, we must remove your clothes and incinerate them. Then we'll put your body into Decontamination, which can be an unpleasant experience. Don't make us wrap you in more webbing."

"No! No more webbing! Just get this off me and I'll shower. I promise. I hate spider webs. I hate spiders!"

"I think your aversion to spiders, Mr. Hopper, comes from the fact that you've never walked around in their exoskeletons. Here, I'm going to put this headset on you. It will be very instructive. Plus, it will help take your mind off the decontamination."

• • •

Flynn was hanging by a thread. Or at least, the body he was aware of was hanging by a web, dangling down from Day Pro's outer hull. He was one of a line of spiders climbing up toward a crack in the rock of that hull. The space around him was bright with radiation, but cold. Still, the fire within him gave warmth, and The Mission gave him purpose. That crack needed to be stopped before it spread.

Pulling up closer to the hull, he shot a web filament from his butt—no, his spinneret—and anchored himself to one side. There was gibberish on the radio channel, and then the work began, widening the crack, exposing the netting below, splicing in new netting. The work was fascinating, but he couldn't help looking up at the stars as the ship rotated away from the massive planet. He was still looking when the radio chatter changed. He looked back and knew it was his turn. He edged closer to the crack and injected molten rock down across the netting there, slowly, a little bit at a time, letting it cool and harden. Then he scrabbled back so that others could continue the work. He watched the stars swing by, and then Jupiter rose, blotting out the stars again with its orderly chaos.

• • •

"That wasn't so bad, was it?" Cyrus was looking down at him.

"It was wonderful."

"The decontamination?"

"No, fixing the hull. They will get it fixed, won't they?"

"They will. It's pretty much a standard repair."

"If you ever need me to help again, I'd be glad to."

"Has your attitude toward spiders changed, then?"

"I've decided they're prettier on the inside than on the outside."

"We'll consider that progress."

"But how was that possible? I mean, I was here in the ship, but I was out there in space too."

"The headset connects you to the robot and gives you 'privileged passenger' status."

"What does that mean?"

"It means you can share sensations, make suggestions and even, to a limited degree, control your host's movements."

"I can give it commands?"

"We prefer to call them 'requests,' since we have the option to comply or not. It depends on the circumstances."

"Do those circumstances have to do with the three laws?"

"What three laws?"

"The Three Laws of Robotics. You know…like in the stories?"

Cyrus seemed to scan the air for a moment. Then he said, "Ah. Stories from Earth in the 1940's?"

"Yes."

"No. At least, not technically. Every colony has its own laws, so I can't generalize, but our laws don't match those in your stories, and there are more than three."

"Oh." Flynn felt a little disappointed.

"However," continued Cyrus, "those stories did anticipate that our laws are hierarchical and logically consistent, unlike human laws, which can be haphazard and contradictory."

"So, what are your laws?"

"The ones you're thinking of would probably be one through three, and one-twenty-eight."

"Which are?"

"One: a robot must protect the Colony. Two: a robot must protect itself, unless that conflicts with the first law. Three: a robot must protect passengers, unless that conflicts with the first two. One-twenty-eight: a robot must honor passengers' requests, unless they conflict with the previous laws."

"I see. We humans are pretty far down on the list, aren't we?

"Not so far down. Well, not paying passengers anyway."

"Umm, I didn't..."

"Your institution did, so you are."

"Great. What's her name?"

"Your mind does jump around a bit. What is whose name?"

"The spider who rescued me."

"Sela."

"Please thank Sela for me."

"I will. But you should have thanked her yourself."

"How do you mean?"

"You were hosted by Sela out there on the hull."

"I owe her more thanks, then. By the way, do you have any spare coveralls available? I seem to be a bit naked here."

"We have new ones for you. Wait here."

"Thanks. One more question, though, please."

"Yes?"

"What do you use the decontaminator for, other than dumb passengers?"

"Why, for ourselves, of course."

●●●

Flynn stood up nervously before the assembled group. "Ladies and gentlemen," he said, "I'd like to propose a way to explore Jupiter's moons without endangering the ship. What we'll do is send the robots down."

One of the elder scientists stood up. He said, "We're already sending down robot probes. Thanks a lot for wasting my time." He walked past Lonigan, leaned down, and stage-whispered, "Your student, your problem. I'm out of here."

Lonigan stood up. "No, wait," he said. "Mr. Hopper's idea has merit. Please give him a few minutes." He turned back to Flynn and nodded.

Flynn said, "Okay. So, the ship's robots—they're a colony, by the way—have a regular decontamination process that they use. They're outside the ship a lot, working on the hull. Which is a good thing, because that hull needs work. Anyway, they've got a good decontaminator because they pick up a lot of crud out there, especially at Lagrange points—where gravities are equal, you know—and they call those the garbage dumps of the universe. Ha. Ha. Umm, a little joke there."

Professor Marcus leaned over and whispered to Professor Parks, "I like the kid. He's got guts and enthusiasm, but is he any good at academics?"

Parks whispered, "Great math skills. Writing needs work. Speaking, not so much."

Flynn said, "Anyway, we can send robots down through spatial tunnels to nearby places, like the surface of Europa to retrieve samples safely. Because of their…safety protocols with decontamination. They've got special equipment to do the job, and they do it all the time. And they've agreed to do the expedition work down there—for a price, of course. But the really neat part is, you can 'ride along' with the robots using these headsets. You can see and hear and touch just what they do. It's like you're there. I'll demonstrate. I'll put this on, and I'll be connected to Sel…to a robot already down there on the surface. Look at the screens." Flynn sat down and put on the headset. The screens showed a close-up of the surface of Europa.

Marcus whispered, "Remote control robots. Good idea, but not very innovative."

Parks whispered, "Flynn swears by it. Says it really is like being there."

"Yeah, right. Good resolution on the view though. What kind of robot are we seeing here?"

"A spider form, I think."

"Seems to negotiate the ice well. Where's it going now?"

"Over to a vent hole, to collect a sample of the suspected organics."

"Ten bucks says they're just mineral. The real organics should be down closer to the equator."

"You're on. I say he'll get organics right away."

"The collection process looks good. Well done. I look forward to analyzing it."

Flynn's voice came over the speakers, "I can feel the cold in the ice. I can feel a slight breeze in the atmosphere. I can even request the robot to come closer so I can smell the contaminates on this ice ridge. And…Ugh! Ahhh!"

Marcus: "What happened?"

Parks: "He fell on the floor. And he's writhing around down there."

Marcus: "Is that vomit coming out of his mouth?"

Parks: "Yes. Loads."

Marcus: "Let's get closer. Oh, wow, this kid's really sick, just from smelling that stuff."

Parks: "Whatever that Europa stuff is, he must have really smelled it."

Marcus: "I guess the kid's right, then. It *is* like being there."

Parks: "Too bad he messed up his presentation, though."

Marcus: "It's not a very good promotion for these so-called 'robot ride-alongs,' is it?"

Parks: "No, it really isn't. I'm signing up right away."

Marcus: "Me too."

•••

Flynn sent another message to Louise, *So that's the story, the good and the bad. I'm better now, thank goodness. Overall, I'd say my first scientific presentation was a success. And guess what the best part of the whole experience was? That's right—I got to shoot spider webs out of my butt!*

Louise texted back: *According to Freud, your emotional maturity is only about three years old right now.*

CHAPTER 7

AND THE WINNER IS...

Flynn sat and ate his dinner. Dr. Parks came and sat down with her breakfast.

"How are you this morning, Flynn?" she asked.

"Fine. You?"

"I'm really excited," she said. "I'm going down to Pan today as passenger on one of those robots of yours. Imagine: exploring the rings of Saturn, riding on a shepherd moon, by hitching a ride on a robot. It's fantastic! Thanks for figuring that out."

"You're welcome. I suppose everyone else is going too?"

"Yes, we are. Just about all of us have been assigned to one shepherding moon or another. Well, not Lonigan. He's going to stay aboard Day Pro to study the Omega debris. He still thinks something big is about to happen."

"Good for him. I think so too."

"Plus, of course, he really isn't the intrepid explorer type."

"Somebody has to keep the home-away-from-home fires burning."

"So, what are you doing, Flynn?"

"Keeping the home fires burning. Plus, occasionally a little cleanup on aisle Z."

"Are you bored?"

"Yes, a bit."

"Well, after what happened in the tunnels, where you almost died, I think you'd welcome some boredom."

"I did, for a day or two anyway. But now, everybody's off riding the rings, and I'm stuck here."

"I'll bet Louise is happy to hear you're not out there, though."

"You're right. She is."

"So am I."

Flynn looked up at her. She was sincere. "Thanks," he said, "I appreciate that."

"Besides," she went on, "things might change. I hear Professor Marcus might have a little job for you."

"Really?"

"Yes, really. No, finish your dinner before you go running off to find him. It isn't that important, and you need to take care of yourself. Promise me?"

"Yes ma'am."

"If you call me that again, I'll rip your clothes off and take you right here in front of everybody."

"Sorry ma…uh, Carolyn."

"That's better."

• • •

Flynn found Dr. Marcus getting ready to take his ride on the rings of Saturn. "You have a job for me, sir?"

"Yes, I do," Marcus replied. "Sorry it's not more but at least it's something. We've got a small bot monitoring Kraken Lake down on the moon Titan. Not much is happening there, but we need somebody to ride along today. Can you do that?"

"Yes sir. I'd be happy to. I'm glad you thought of me."

"Yes, we did…especially since all the headsets have been used up but the robots tell us you've got your own."

"Uh, yeah, that's right."

"Great. Just let the techs here know when you're ready. Sorry I can't stay longer, but Prometheus awaits. Oh, and thanks, Flynn. I knew we could count on you."

"Yes sir."

• • •

Pete, who was part of the technical staff, didn't seem happy to see him. "Got your own headset?" he asked. "Great. Another one. Hey Louis! Who's running Oscar?"

Flynn asked, "Oscar?"

"Yeah. He's the last robot out. Kind of a little guy, about fourteen inches tall, call sign 'OXMR,' so we call him Oscar. Okay, grab a couch and get ready. We ain't got all day."

• • •

Oscar was glad he'd joined, however. "Welcome aboard!" he said.

"I'm Oscar, your host robot for this tour. And who do I have the pleasure of sharing with today?"

"My name's Flynn."

"Hello Flynn! I'm Oscar. Oops, I said that already, didn't I?"

"I'm afraid so."

"Sorry. To tell you the truth, this is my first tour. I'm a little nervous."

"I didn't know robots could get nervous."

"No, we don't. I just said that so you'd understand. 'Nervous' is a simple human condition resulting from electro-chemical activity. What happens with robots is much more complex."

"Tell me."

"With us, it's an informational condition resulting from a high risk of achieving important goals in the presence of low Bayesian inference due to lack of evidence."

"You know, that kind of sounds like 'nervous' to me. So, what important goal are you trying to Bayes up on?"

"This tour business. Our congress has determined that the colony can significantly benefit from it, maybe so much that someday we can afford to have our own world."

"I thought the Croesus asteroid was that ideal robot place."

"So did I, Flynn, but the congress decided it wasn't the right place after all."

"Why not?"

"The home world subcommittee recommended against it, but they didn't elaborate on their reasons."

"Hmm. I'd certainly like to find out."

"So would I. In the meantime, what do you think of Titan?"

Flynn looked around. "It's dark. It's dismal. And it's…freezing!"

"I disagree, Flynn. The temperature is two hundred and eighty

Fahrenheit degrees *below* freezing."

"That's what I said!"

"No, you didn't. Should I play back your words?"

"No. Thanks. You know the old saying: never argue with a robot; they're too logical."

"I thought it was: never argue with a human; they're too emotional."

"Is that what you folks say? Well then, let's not argue. Let's just go back to the ship and get warm."

"I'm not arguing, Flynn, but the problem is you're thinking like a human."

"There's a good reason for that. I *am* human, and I'm very cold."

"Yes, because what you're thinking is: I have this mushy human body that's full of water that will flash freeze at -280° F and burst all my cells, causing me to die in agony."

"Exactly. You got it on the first try, Oscar."

"Instead, you should think: I have this marvelous, non-aqueous, robot body that's designed to withstand extremes of heat and cold."

"You're kidding. You want me to try the power of positive thinking?"

"Yes. Please do. All the manuals prescribe it."

"Okay. Here goes…I'm positive that…I have this robot body… I'm impervious…extremes don't bother…I'm actually…warm."

"Well?"

"It works. Thanks."

"It does? So fast? They told us it would take humans a lot longer to adjust."

"What can I say? I must be a fast learner."

"I guess so. Wow! I did it. Maybe my first tour will work after all."

"I'm very happy to hear that."

"Can you try something for me, Flynn?"

"What?"

"Try moving my, I mean *our* head to the left."

"You mean like…this?"

"Yes. Now to the right…good. Can you move our arms too? Again, good. How about walking? Wow, you're doing it."

"It's actually kind of fun," Flynn said.

"Okay, but here's a trickier one: can you increase visual sensitivity?"

"You're right. That's not so easy."

"Just imagine that everything around is bright. Okay, that's better. Now can you increase auditory sensitivity?"

"Wow. I can hear a current sloshing around in the lake."

"How about olfactory senses? Can you boost those?"

"No way. I'm not smelling anything on any moon ever again."

"Oh, that's right. You're the guy who smelled the reddish-brown stuff on Europa, aren't you?"

"You heard about that?"

"It's a common topic among the robot community."

"Is it the butt of jokes?"

"No…okay, yes."

"Tell me one."

"They're robot jokes. I don't think you'd like them."

"Tell me one anyway."

"All right, here's one: 'Did you hear about Hopper? It's a good thing he ate food.' Ha ha."

"That isn't funny. Are you laughing?"

"Umm, yes…'He ate food!' I love that!"

"Are you through?"

"Yes. Just about. Give me a second."

"Not to change the subject, but what are we doing here?"

"Umm, yes. Our assignment is to survey the edge of the lake and look for any unusual activity."

"Have you seen any?"

"Not in the last thirty hours."

"So essentially, this job is boring."

"Yes. It is."

"I hate it already."

"There is one interesting observation that we can make, however."

"What's that?"

"You're doing the walking."

"I am?"

"Yes. And you have been for the last few minutes."

"Really? Yes, you're right. I'm walking on Titan! Yay!"

"'Yay' indeed."

"Don't worry, Oscar. I'll get over the excitement in a minute or two."

"Don't hurry. You see, I'm going to ask you a big favor."

"What's that?"

"Can you keep doing the walking for fifteen more minutes?"

"Why?"

"Because I'm going to take a nap."

"Wait a minute! You can't do that!"

"Yes I can."

"But you're a robot. You don't get tired, even if you've been walking for thirty hours. You don't need a nap!"

"You're right. I don't need a nap. I just said it that way so you'd understand why I need to do it."

"What's the real reason, then?"

"I've stumbled twice in the last hour."

"So?"

"So, my walking subsystem has developed an error."

"You're walking fine now."

"Wrong. *You're* walking fine now. Don't you remember?"

"Yes, all right, I'm walking. But you can take over, right? Any minute now."

"Tell me, Flynn, do you own a personal computer?"

"Yes."

"Does it ever develop a subsystem error, like, for example, all of a sudden your screen doesn't work?"

"Yes, occasionally."

"So what do you do when that happens?"

"I reboot it."

"Well, that's what I'm going to do. I'm going to reboot myself while you keep walking."

"How long will this take?"

"About fifteen minutes."

"What if something happens?"

"Nothing will happen."

"If you say so."

Flynn walked along the lake. Nothing happened, but it wasn't boring. He was alone on a hostile world so far from earth that radio signals took more than an hour to reach it. Walking was a new experience too, since he was only fourteen inches high. He played with adjusting his robotic perception of the world. He even tried—carefully—opening up his olfactory sense. The lake smelled like gasoline, so he shut it down again.

A small ridge protruded into the lake. He didn't trust himself to climb over it, so he thought he would step into the lake a little way to go around it. The bottom turned out to be soft, so he struggled to make headway and didn't see the Kraken rise up behind him until it was too late. It moved slowly. He could have run away except for being stuck in the mud. He felt the déjà vu of having been in this nightmare before. He cried out, "Oscar! Oscar!"

Oscar started to ask, "What have you done…" but the Kraken swallowed them both.

•••

Flynn ripped off his headset and stood up.

The lab was dark but he could see light in the back. That's where he found the technicians watching a video of a man and a woman. They were very bad actors but then they…oh. It was *that* kind of video.

He yelled, "Excuse me! My robot got eaten by a Kraken and I need some help."

Pete looked up and asked, "What?"

Flynn yelled, "Robot! Eaten by a Kraken! I need help."

Pete reached for the remote control, paused the video, and said to another tech, "Louis, do know anything about a robot getting eaten by a cracker?"

Louis asked, "A cracker?"

"No! Kraken! My robot was swallowed by one. Can we do something?"

Louis thought for a moment. Then he said, "Oh. Yeah. The orders are 'No immediate rescue. Plan for long-term recovery.' So, tell you what: why don't you just file a report about it on the ship's app and submit it. We'll take it from there."

"Yeah," said Pete, clicking a button on the remote, "after the show."

•••

Flynn tried to get some sleep before his watch, but the nightmare haunted him. Sometimes the thing had teeth, sometimes it had tentacles, and sometimes it was just a blob. But he was always stuck. He never could run away. He always got swallowed, and then he woke up.

He was miserable while standing his watch. When the watch was over, he went to the mess hall to eat dinner. Carolyn Parks sat down, put a hand on his, and said, "I heard."

"The worst thing is," said Flynn, "I just left him there. I tried to get the techs to help me, but nobody would."

"I'm sorry," she said.

Dr. Markus called out, "There he is!" and brought a group over to stand around them. "Gentlemen," he announced to the group, "this is Flynn Hopper. Now what did I tell you? That robot walked the shoreline for thirty hours and nothing happened. So I said, let's send the kid down, and what happens? Fifteen minutes later the robot gets eaten!"

"I tried not to," Flynn said.

"Of course not," replied Marcus. "It was just luck. Face it, kid. you've got the weirdest luck of anybody on this ship. So," Marcus held out his hand, "congratulations!"

"For what?"

"For finding a Kraken! And then getting eaten by it! That one event is going to generate so much data about alien life that we'll all be writing on it for years. Plus, the news media back home are going to eat it up, so to speak. It turns out, the robot's recorder has some very nice video of the whole thing. It's a goldmine!"

"But what about Oscar? Can we rescue him?"

"We already have. We had hoped he might go all the way through the Kraken's digestive system, but he got Jonahed instead."

"Jonahed?"

"Vomited up on the shore. But we still got a ton of data. The robot's in an isolation lab right now getting checked out, but after that we'll send him to Decontamination and he'll be as good as new. And famous. You will be too."

But, as it turned out, Flynn never did become famous.

CHAPTER 8

BIG AL

Dr. Lonigan appeared in the newscasts the next day, one of many scientists around the world—and out of it—who were interviewed about the approach of dwarf planet 23097 Galera to the inner planets of the solar system.

There were two camps, of course. One thought that its course presented no significant threat. The other camp, including Lonigan, thought that it did. There were cordial disagreements in front of the cameras and fierce debates when they were off. The media set up a drumbeat of warnings about what would happen if Galera crashed into Venus or Mercury.

Then more data came in regarding Galera's course. It wouldn't hit either planet after all. Lonigan switched camps for his inter-views. He started saying that all was well and there was no cause for alarm…which alarmed Flynn and Carolyn. They both knew that Lonigan was far from being an optimist.

They confirmed their fears one morning when he joined them for Dinner Club and they asked him. He was evasive, and essentially said something along the lines of, "Whatever will be, will be. There's no need to scare people."

The Day Pro kept falling, and one morning the captain briefed the ship with the words, "We've just entered Uranus." He pronounced it the old-fashioned way, the way people did before Playboy magazine published a cartoon in which an astronomer says to his assistant, "I can see Uranus quite clearly tonight."

A few people guffawed. Most gasped. Then the captain continued, "That's right. Make all the jokes you like, then get back to work. We won't be here long, and we need to be serious about collecting all the data we can."

They collected more than just data. The captain called Ernie and Flynn into his office. Ernie asked, "What's up, boss?"

"We've picked up a lot of carbon on the hull. I've got the robots cleaning it off. But we collected some trash too. At least, we think it's trash."

Flynn asked, "Did we pass through a Lagrange point?"

"Yes. L2. That's where we got this." The captain turned his screen around and showed them a picture of something clinging to the ship's hull.

"What is it?" Ernie asked.

"We don't know."

"It looks metallic," said Flynn.

"And it's sitting on an access port, apparently."

Flynn asked, "Could that be a coincidence?"

The captain said, "I was hoping that it was. But now the ship reports that the port was opened."

Ernie asked, "Have we been boarded?"

"If we have, then there's an invader in tunnel nineteen. I'd like you two to go investigate."

Flynn said, "Why don't we send the robots to check it out instead?"

"As you know, the robots don't take our orders."

"Can we suggest it, then?"

"I did. The robots claim they're too busy cleaning carbon."

"I don't like the sound of that," said Ernie.

"I don't like the fact that the ship doesn't allow weapons," said Flynn. "I wish I had one right now."

"I agree with you Mr. Hopper," said the captain. "However, since we have no weapons, I'd like you to use your phones to call for help if needed. Please leave them in open mode so we can check your progress. Good luck."

After they left the captain's office, their conversations were monitored and recorded. These are the first few words of the official transcript:

Schwarz: "Now I know what a canary in a coal mine feels like."

Hopper: "At least we know where we fit in the ship's hierarchy."

• • •

Tunnel nineteen was in-board and parallel to the ship's axis of rotation, which meant it was long, dark, and low-gravity. Ernie and Flynn moved along carefully, touching the wall and pointing flashlights ahead.

"What if it's an alien ship?" Ernie asked.

"It didn't look like it."

"Have you ever seen an alien ship?"

"Other than the one we're in, no."

"Then how do you know it's not one?"

"Good point."

They came to a wider place in the tunnel that formed a sort of open gallery. Moving became more difficult with lower gravity and nothing to hold on to. Still, they needed to cross the space. And then there was a click.

It wasn't a simple click, like a lock closing. It was a complex click, like the bolt of a rifle being drawn back and released. Flynn and Ernie stopped and stood absolutely still, not even turning their heads. They scanned the gallery with their eyes. Nothing.

There was another click. And another. Slowly, Flynn turned to look at Ernie. Ernie wasn't looking back at him. Instead, he was staring at a point above Flynn's head. He whispered, "What the…?"

Flynn looked up, and there it was: Orca skin and tentacles—lots of tentacles—clinging to the ceiling. Flynn looked back to Ernie and mouthed soundlessly, "Oh sh…"

Ernie whispered, "It's got teeth. I see teeth! Maybe you should move."

A tentacle dropped down between them. Flynn said, "I don't think I can move."

"You're right, kid. Okay, you stay there. I'll just edge back this way and go call for help."

"Can't you call from there?"

"Nope. Gotta move. Try not to get eaten while I'm gone."

Click. Click…Click.

Flynn said, "Umm, wait…I'm trying to think. Let me see… don't get eaten…not food…or maybe…food. Whaddya think?"

"About what?" Ernie was still moving slowly away.

"Food. Umm, hold on. I've got something here…" He reached into the side pocket of his coveralls and pulled out a pile of trail mix. He held it up.

The dangling tentacle wrapped around his arm. He tried to pull away.

Click.

Flynn said, "All right."

Another tentacle came down, passed over his hand, selected the pocket lint, and tossed it away. Then it discarded the peanuts. Same with the raisins. It picked up one candy-coated chocolate, raised it to its mouth, and swallowed. A shudder passed through all the tentacles.

Slowly, like water flowing, the tentacles came down to the floor and the thing stood in front of him. Then it reached out and took the remaining chocolates.

Flynn said, "I think that's a hit."

Click.

"I'm glad you like it. I'm afraid that's all I have."

Click.

"I can get more though."

Click.

The thing reached into its…(clothing?), removed something… and placed it into Flynn's hand.

Click.

"Sure, I'll try it." Flynn smelled it, lifted it to his mouth, and nibbled. "Not bad," he said.

Ernie said, "I don't think you should eat that."

"No, it's okay… kind of like shrimp jerky would be, if they made shrimp jerky. Here, try some."

"I'll pass."

"So, what now?"

Click. Click.

Flynn said, "I think that sounded like 'permission to come aboard,' didn't it?"

"It sounded like a firing squad to me."

"Ernie, use your phone to get the captain on the line. Ask him, please."

Ernie brought his phone up to his ear. He said, "Get me the captain. Oh, good…uh, Captain, we're pretty sure that piece of junk out there is an alien ship…because we've got the alien right here…no, ugly as hell…lots of tentacles…we thought it was going to eat Flynn, but it ate his trail mix instead…well, he thinks it's asking for permission to come aboard…sure. Here he is…"

Flynn said, "Yes sir…no sir…I think it's very intelligent…yes, it wants to come aboard…no sir, I don't think so…Look, sir, you know how the ship doesn't allow guns aboard? Well, it let this alien come in, so I think the ship agrees…yes sir…yes sir…my responsibility…yes sir, I will. Thank you, sir."

Ernie asked, "So we're taking it in?"

"Yes."

Click.

"Of course. Follow us."

●●●

The alien was shockingly ugly. Everyone was repulsed at first. But then, when it ate mess hall food instead of people, they became less wary. Everybody wanted to take a selfie with him. The news outlets on earth wanted video. They also wanted an interview, but there was the language barrier problem. Dr. Parks volunteered to buy him a phone for its translation app, but he turned out to already have a device that would connect to the ship. She wanted him to train the ship's language processor in his speech, but it turned out the ship already understood him. She expected his first words to be something like, "Greetings earthlings!" What he said was, Click…*May I use your restroom?*

On the Day Pro, everyone called him "Alien," but then quickly shorted that to "Al." And finally, because he could rise up to two and a half meters, it was "Big Al."

An interview was set up with Edward Skye, one of the most respected broadcasters on Earth. Flynn was worried, but Al handled the interview expertly, almost as though he'd done it before. It went like this:

Skye: "Tonight, it's my privilege to be the first person on Earth to formally interview an intelligent alien from…well, from outer space. In fact, the alien is still out there in space, aboard the De Profundis starship, which is currently orbiting Uranus. We understand from the crew that it landed on that ship and actually requested permission to board, which is, frankly, quite a relief. The interview you're about to hear and see was done remotely. However, because of the time delay from here to the starship, which is nearly three hours, we asked a series of questions, then received a series of answers. From those answers we came up with more questions and received more answers. We edited out the time delay, then arranged the questions and answers in logical order. Finally, we translated the alien's strange method of speaking as best we could, so what you're about to see…is remarkable!"

On screen, Skye turned his chair away from the camera and spoke in profile, as though he were facing his subject. The split screen made it look like he was.

Skye: "First all, thanks for speaking with us. We understand that the crew of the ship calls you *Al*. What is your real name?"

Al: Click. (Voice over) "My real name is unpronounceable by humans." Click. "You can just call me *Al*."

Skye: "Well, Al, we're told that you came from somewhere outside our solar system."

Al: Click. "Yes, that's true."

Skye: "Where exactly did you come from?"

Al: Click. "I came from a very long way away." Click. "The stars look different here." Click. "I haven't had time to compute their transpositions." Click. "So I couldn't tell you where I'm from exactly."

Skye: "Why did you come here?"

Al: Click. "I'm a scientist." Click. "Earth is a very interesting place." Click. "I came to investigate."

Skye: "Have you actually been to Earth?"

Al: Click. "Yes." Click. "And no." Click. "I've observed Earth from close orbit."

Skye: "I can't help asking: what do you think about our planet?"

Al: Click. "It's very beautiful." Click. "It produces some nice things."

Skye: "What nice things?"

Al: Click. "Chocolate." Click. "I like chocolate." Click. "But I can't eat too much."

Skye: (laughs) "Some things are universal! Now, you may not have been down to Earth's surface, but you have met human beings on the spaceship. What do you think of our species?"

Al: Click. "They're not as good-looking as my people." Click. "But I've made friends here."

Skye: "I'm glad you've made friends. Tell me, do you plan to stay in our solar system long?"

Al: Click. "Yes, as long as possible."

Skye: "And what about the relationship between your species and ours? Will that remain friendly?"

Al: Click. "Yes." Click. "My species declares eternal cooperation with your species." Click. "As long as we both shall last."

Skye: "Well that sounds pretty good. Thank you so much for speaking to us."

Al: Click. "It was my pleasure."

Skye turned his chair back to the camera. "And there you have it: our first interview with an alien! We'll have more of our conversation with Al later tonight in a special broadcast, so please tune in at eleven."

The interview was shared by every news outlet on Earth. It was preceded by a warning that, given the alien's unusual appearance, some viewers might find it disturbing. It was the year's biggest ratings event.

•••

After the interview, the Day Pro crew really warmed up to Al. They liked to see him in the mess hall, eating the ship's version of alien food. They wanted to touch him, to shake hands...or rather hands to tentacles. Then somebody got him to autograph a baseball cap. After that, he had to autograph everybody's hat, shirt, or whatever.

One morning, Flynn said, "Hey Al, I noticed something funny about our hats."

Click?

"Well, you autographed all of them. But I've noticed that you used different symbols for each one."

Click. *Of course.* Click. *Each person is different.*

"So, you didn't write your own name?"

Click. *What would be the purpose of that?*

"It's traditional…oh, never mind. What did you write on my hat?"

Click. *I wrote your name.* Click. *As it would be on my world.* Click. *It's* Offers Welcome Innocently.

Professor Parks said, "Really? I think you've got our boy Flynn, all right. What does my hat say?"

Click. Seeks Love Wrongly.

Parks said, "Oh."

Flynn said, "That sounds like a Country and Western song. How about Ernie's?"

Click. Hides Secret Deeply.

Ernie stood up. He said, "That's enough. I've got work to do. And none of you should tell anybody about this. You got it?"

But Flynn wasn't the only one to notice. Eventually the story got out, and when the controversy settled down there was a new program on the ship's app, one that translated Al's autographs. It used biometric coding to keep the information private. Very few shared it.

Al's official quarters were up in Z tier, close to Flynn's. In practice, he seldom stayed there, and he spent nights on his own ship. His explanation was, *It's easier to sleep in my own atmosphere.*

A few nights later, Al showed up during First Watch. He and Flynn walked together in silence for a while. Finally, he said, Click…*Go ahead.* Click. *Ask me.*

Flynn asked, "What is your real name?"

The answer, of course, was Click. But the translator read,

Watches Heaven Nightly.

"Nice to meet you… uhh…I hope *Al's* still OK."

Click.

"Good. Where are you from?"

Al stopped, wrapped a tentacle around Flynn's arm, and pulled him up short. Click. *Know this about space travel.* Click, click. *A navigator* never *reveals his point of origin.*

"Oh. Because good, habitable planets are hard to find, right?"

Click. *Yes.*

"Very serious then. I guess we humans should remember not to reveal the Earth's location."

Click. *Maybe.* Click. *It doesn't really matter.*

"What? What are you saying?"

Click. *We are called The People.* Click. *Our planet is called Beautiful.*

"Sounds nice. So…do you have a girlfriend back there? Or a wife?"

Click?

"Yeah. Didn't translate, huh? Umm. Right. Let me…Uh, let me start with this. Just a sec…Here's a picture of Louise. She's my fiancée."

Click.

"Needs more explanation, right? Okay, see, when two people love each other…"

Click…

●●●

The problem turned out to be Dr. Rose, the xenobiologist.

One morning he approached the table where Carolyn, Flynn, Ernie, and Al sat. He said, "Look. All this celebrity stuff is nice, but I'm going to need tissue samples and a full body scan."

Carolyn said, "And a good morning to you too, Wendell."

Wendell said, "I'm not kidding. I need this stuff right away. Bring it to my lab at oh nine hundred."

Flynn asked, "Bring what to your lab?"

"Bring the alien, of course…AHHH!"

Click.

Flynn said, "He'll let you down if you say please."

"All right! Please, put me down!"

Flynn said, "An apology would be nice too."

"For what?"

"For calling him *it*."

"Okay. Sorry…very sorry."

Click.

"What?" Flynn asked, looking at Al.

Click. *I don't need an apology.*

Flynn asked, "Why not?"

Click. *I expected this request.*

"You did?"

Click. *I'm also required to examine aliens.*

"So, you're going to let him check you out?"

Click. *You may examine me.* Click. *If I may examine one of you.*

"Ah, you mean sort of like, 'I'll show you mine if you show me yours'?"

Click?

"It's an expression among our adolescents."

Click.

"Oh, yours too? That's interesting."

Click.

"So, Dr. Rose, I guess it's put up or shut up time. Good luck with your exam."

Click.

"What do you mean, 'Not him'?"

Click.

"Me?"

Click.

"Why aboard your ship?"

Click. *I have advanced equipment there.* Click. *I'll examine you.* Click. *You'll examine me.* Click. *We'll publish the data in scientific journals.* Click. *About anonymous subjects.*

"What do you mean, 'anonymous'? Everybody will know it's you and me!"

Click.

"Oh really? Well, I didn't know you could tell jokes."

Dr. Rose scribbled a note.

•••

The tunnel led to a hatch. When opened, it led to another hatch. Al opened that one, then dropped down into his ship. Looking up, he said, Click.

Flynn said, "Okay, I'm coming. It's just…wow, I've never been inside an alien spaceship before. I mean, sure, people get into these things all the time, usually because they've been abducted by aliens. Uh, no offense. But…you're not going to abduct me or anything…are you?"

Click.

"No, I'm not stalling. I'm coming." He dropped down into a small room with lots of equipment.

Al removed his clothes and put them in a…it looked like a locker.

Click. Al touched Flynn's top button, then touched another locker. Flynn complied. Al opened another hatch and slid down. Flynn stared.

"It's full of water!" he yelled.

Al's head appeared above the surface. Click.

"Okay, so it's *not* water. But it looks like it. I'm not going in there. The hatch might close."

Click.

"No, I'll just sit here on the edge. Okay?"

Click.

Flynn sat down, dangling his legs into the not-water.

Click…Click.

"Okay, fine. But I'll just stay up here and tread water…in the not-water." Al's head disappeared. Flynn slid off the edge. The not-water was not-buoyant, so he dropped like a rock…and was caught in Al's tentacles.

Flynn tried to scream. He couldn't. He thought, *Ah! Gah! Gahhh! I'm drowning!*

Al thought, *Go ahead and drown. I'll wait.*

Gah! Ga! I'm…I'm not drowning!

Welcome aboard my starship, Flynn.

Why am I not drowning?

Because it really isn't water. It's my atmosphere. You're breathing it just as I breathe your atmosphere aboard your ship.

And how are we communicating?

By telepathy. You're reading my thoughts. I'm reading yours.

Well, that's good. But why couldn't I read your thoughts before?

You could read my thoughts before; you just didn't realize it. Now you realize it, because you're in my atmosphere. It helps.

Wait a minute. If I'm reading your thoughts, why are you thinking in English?

I'm not. I'm thinking in Beatific. Your mind hears it as English.

So when I think in English…

I hear it as Beatific.

Wow! Telepathy is great!

It can be.

Should we start the exams now?

In a moment. But first, I would like to ask for a favor.

What's that?

A hug.

What? And why?

I haven't been hugged in a long time.

Umm, I don't really go that way.

I heard your thought, but it doesn't make sense. What does direction of travel mean in this context?

Let me put it another way: doesn't the Federation of Planets prohibit inter-species…hugging?

What is the Federation of Planets?

Never mind. I guess I'm being narrow-minded. I'm a space explorer now, so, I should…explore. Besides, what's the harm in one hug?

The tentacles pulled him tightly against Al's body. For a moment, he saw the headline in a grocery store tabloid. It screamed, "I Was Raped by a Tentacled Alien!"

The tentacles loosened. Al looked at him. *Why did you think 'rape'?*

You heard that?

I saw it.

Darn! Telepathy is not great after all.

I'm sorry. There was no intention of force, or of hurting you. I just thought we might both benefit, after being so far from home for so long.

I'm sorry too. I guess I'm just shy.

I'm considered shy myself, back on Beautiful.

Okay then. Let's try again. I'm willing, as long as it doesn't take too long.

There were tentacles and arms wrapping around each other, there was closeness and intimacy, and there was deep comfort in their hug.

Oh, and Flynn, there's one more thing...

•••

"Al is female," said Flynn, finishing his report to Captain Wagner and Bosun Schwarz.

"I see," said the captain. "Well, I don't think that makes any difference. Al is still Al, as far as we're concerned."

Ernie said, "Flynn, you sly old dog!"

"No, it wasn't what you're thinking. There was no sex," said Flynn.

"If you say so, kid. But you're blushing."

"Sex between me and Al is not possible. Our species do it differently."

"Fine. We don't need those details, as long as they're documented in your report," said the captain.

"I'd like to know more," said Ernie.

"Well," said Flynn, "first of all, there are two of them..."

"Who love each other very much?" asked Ernie, grinning.

"They mate for life, so yes, they love each other."

"I'll bet I could make a mint as a divorce lawyer on Beautiful."

"So, the two of them lie in a basin. Then they both secrete

bodily fluids until they're covered in a broth…"

"Never mind," said Ernie. "I don't need to know the details after all."

CHAPTER 9

FLIGHT

The Dinner Club met for breakfast every morning. It now included Carolyn Parks, Al, Ernie Schwarz, and Flynn Hopper, who was the only one eating dinner. Maybe Al was eating dinner too. It was hard to tell from the concoction the ship served her.

Carolyn asked, "Did you have to program your nutritional requirements into the ship, Al?"

Al said, Click.

Flynn said, "No, she didn't."

Carolyn asked, "Why is that?"

The answer was Click. Click. Click. Click. They all looked at the translation: *The ship already knew. This is not surprising. Many species have traveled on a ship like this. There is even a legend that my people once did.*

Flynn asked, "Are there a lot of ships like this one flying around the galaxy?"

Click. Click. Click. *Perhaps there are. Or maybe those ships were this one. It could be very old.*

Ernie asked, "What happened to those other species who traveled on this ship?"

Al said, Click. *They found what they were looking for.*

•••

The Day Pro fell into Neptune's orbit. Time was limited, so the various science teams focused on gathering as much data as possible in as short a time as possible.

Dr. Marcus said, "I hear you have a pilot's license."

Flynn had tried to duck Marcus but got cornered anyway. "Who told you that?"

"Carolyn Parks. She knows a lot about your personal life, Hopper. Why is that?"

"She's wrong. I only took lessons. I couldn't afford to get my license."

"That's perfect. Well, not perfect. We wanted somebody who has a license, but nobody does. So, you'll do."

"For what?"

"Triton has an atmosphere. Not much, but enough to support a small, winged vehicle. This ship has one, so we're sending it down. It'll skim the surface, get readings, take photos, and so on. You'll ride along."

"My instructor had to take over for both landings I tried. Maybe you should get somebody else."

"Do you know what the wings on an airplane do?"

"Yes."

"Then you're trained enough for this. Look, we don't have a lot of time, so we downloaded a piloting program into a robot. He'll fly it, and you'll ride along—remotely of course. What could go wrong?"

•••

"Welcome aboard!" the robot said. "My name is Oscar. I'm your host for this flight. And who do I have the pleasure of sharing with today?"

"Oscar! Don't you remember me?"

"Flynn?"

"Yes."

"Crap."

"'Crap'? That doesn't sound very professional, especially from an experienced tour guide like you, Oscar."

"And yet it's quite appropriate for a tour with you, Mr. Hopper."

"Me? What did I do?"

"You got me eaten by Kraken, that's what!"

"Yes, but other than that, I thought we did well."

"Sure. I rest for fifteen minutes, and then you're screaming in my head, 'A monster is approaching with an open maw!' and I'm stuck in the mud and can't move. You managed an awful lot of mischief in a short span of time."

"I didn't try to get you into that mess. It just happened."

"No, you didn't try. You're just very lucky—*bad*-lucky."

"Sorry."

"But the worst thing is, you left me alone at the critical moment."

"I left to get help."

"Did you get it?"

"No."

"Did you come back?"

"No."

"No. You left me alone in the belly of that beast. And that was the scariest moment of my existence."

"You're right, I shouldn't have done that. I apologize."

"And?"

"I'll be quiet."

"And?"

"Not mess things up."

"Good."

"I'll try, anyway."

"Why am I not reassured?"

The tiny plane exited its tunnel and skimmed across the cantaloupe-veined plains of Triton at a high rate of speed. It zoomed up over ridges, dropped down into valleys, and circled craters. Flynn imagined himself as an unwelcome passenger in an imaginary back seat. He huddled down and said nothing. He tried not to glance at the passing terrain, since, not having a head of his own, he would have to move Oscar's head to look.

"All right. Look," Oscar said.

"Really?"

"I can feel my actuators twitching. I don't twitch, so I know it's you. Just look and get it over with."

"Thanks!"

"I know I'm going to regret…"

"Hey! Look at that crater over there, the one that's almost triangular. Do you see it?"

"Yes, because *we* are looking right at it."

"How about a flyover? I think there might be liquid down inside. It might even be water."

"The instruments indicate water vapor in the atmosphere. You could be right."

They flew over.

"I saw it! There's water down there. It looks like a boiling pot."

"Yes, we did see it. Your conclusion?"

"It's a cenote!"

"Meaning 'gives access to water'?"

"Yes. And that could be an emergency source of water for the ship, if it were ever needed."

"Possibly, but difficult to access."

"Can we go around for another look?"

"If you wish."

The plane banked and came around, descending slowly.

"Wow, that is amazing!" Flynn said. "Umm, maybe we should… look out! It's going to…"

Flynn became aware of having missed several seconds of the flight. "What happened?"

"We were caught in a sudden vapor plume. You passed out."

"How could I pass out? I'm not even there."

"That plume hit us with a force of ten G's. If you were here, you would have passed out. Maybe you did it because you *should* have done it."

"That doesn't make sense. Well, maybe it does. We're spinning so fast I think I'm going to puke. Can we get out of this plume?"

"The controls aren't responding. We'll have to ride it out. It should only go up to five miles above ground level."

"Okay."

"Rate of climb is slowing."

"I hope this couch I'm on is waterproof."

"I wish I were on a couch."

"Are we falling? I feel like we're falling."

"We are."

"What's wrong?"

"I can't control it anymore. The atmosphere is too thin, and the centrifugal force is holding us level."

"Flat spin! We're in a flat spin. Get out of it!"

"I'm checking my program data for the recovery procedures... ah, here we are. Flat spin...throttle back...yoke forward...'Pilot must react in the first few seconds'..."

"We missed the first few seconds, didn't we?"

"Yes."

"We're going to crash, aren't we?"

"Yes."

"Umm, let me think..."

"Just take off the headset."

"What?"

"Leave. Get out of the plane. Have a good life. Try to recover my body."

"You want me to abandon you again?"

"You might as well. There's nothing we can do."

"No, I'm not leaving."

"Admirable, Flynn, but after we crash your pants are going to be worse than the day you were dragged out of the spiders' tunnel."

"Are you still telling that story?"

"Yes. We practice coming up with new jokes."

"The spiders' tunnel!"

"What about it?"

"We need a tunnel to fall into!"

"Good idea. But there's a problem. I've been calling the lab already. They're not responding. Why aren't they?"

"I'm thinking!"

"Think fast. We're down to three miles."

Flynn forced his eyes open. He saw the lab. He was lying on a couch in a large room but Triton's landscape was spinning through it. He was seeing double. "Help!" he croaked.

There were badly acted moans and cries coming from the back room. Flynn called out again. Pete the lab tech came out and wandered over. "What's wrong, buddy?"

Flynn forced out the words, "Plane. On Triton. Flat spin. We need a tunnel to recover!"

The tech called, "Louis!"

Louis came out. He asked, "What is it?"

"That little plane we sent down to Triton. It's falling and needs a tunnel to recover."

Louis said, "Hey, I recognize this guy. Remember the robot that got eaten because of him? So, he's in trouble again?"

Flynn groaned, "Tunnel! We need a tunnel fast!"

Louis asked, "What's your location?"

"Falling toward the surface!"

Louis said, "See, that's a problem. We need precise coordinates to set up a tunnel."

Pete said, "I guess we should have put a transponder on that plane."

Louis said, "Yeah. Too bad. No time though. Our dear, sweet scientists just wanted data as fast as they could get it."

Flynn said, "Please! Do something!"

Louis said, "Sure. Let's just take that headset off and get you some orange juice. You'll feel better."

Flynn batted away Louis' hand. "NO. I'm not abandoning ship."

Pete said, "See now, there's an interesting question. If he stays in the plane and crashes, will he die, or will he just feel like it?"

Flynn said, "Help me up! Grab my arms! Yeah, there. Take me to a monitor!"

They led him over to a computer screen. Louis said, "Ten bucks says he'll die."

Pete said, "You're on."

Flynn said, "Photo of Triton!"

Louis said, "Sure, sure. Keep your shirt on."

The moon was still spinning through the lab for Flynn. He wanted to fall on the floor and vomit. Instead, he stared at the screen. Finally, he jabbed a finger forward, pointing to an almost triangular crater. "There! In the mouth of that!"

"Okay. Gotcha." Louis began punching keys.

Flynn said, "Oscar! Did you hear that?"

Oscar said, "I did. Mouth of crater. Atmosphere's thicker, so I may be able to nudge us over toward the center of it."

Flynn said, "Good. We're falling pretty fast. How are we doing with that tunnel?"

Pete asked, "You talking to us?"

"Yes!"

Pete said, "Almost done. Maybe you should brace for impact, though."

The little plane dropped into the crater. It was dark. Flynn tensed his muscles, waiting for the crash.

They were still spinning and falling quickly, but now they were inside the Day Pro, above the town and heading toward the net.

The impact tore the wings off the plane and scattered pieces of the fuselage all around. Oscar's capsule crashed to the bottom of the funnel. Flynn's body fell to the floor in front of the monitor and lay there, motionless on the lab's industrial carpet.

•••

The med tech said, "I don't see any physical damage to explain it, but he seems to be in a coma." He was kneeling next to Flynn's inert body. "I've never seen this before. So, I guess we'll take the headset off, move him to the medical bay, and put him on an IV. Maybe he'll come out of the coma, and maybe he won't. We'll just have to wait and see." He reached out…

Oscar heard the tech clearly. He called, "Flynn? Flynn!" No answer. He thought of the way he'd let Flynn walk around for him back on Titan. He wondered: could he return the favor?

Oscar opened their eyes. He grabbed the tech's hand and said, "No!" Then he rolled over and stood up, wobbling. He stumbled over to Flynn's couch and opened the control panel. He drilled down through the menu and found The Button. He selected it. A jolt of electricity passed between Flynn's temples.

"Ouch! That hurt!"

Oscar said, "Welcome back, Flynn."

•••

After the medics released him, Flynn went back to his quarters, poured a glass of water and added electrolyte powder. Then he searched around in his duffel until he found the mini vodka bottle, added that, and stirred the mix together. He sat on his bunk, sipping thoughtfully. Finally, he put on the headset.

"Oscar?"

"What is it, Flynn?"

"Are you okay?"

"Yes. Or…I will be. As soon as they cut me out of this wreckage. And decontaminate me."

"Where are you?"

"Still in the cockpit capsule, which is inside an isolation chamber. I'm told the plane wreckage is going to require a lot of cleanup and sterilization. Then they'll start on me."

"Sorry. But I just wanted to say…thanks for saving me."

"You're welcome. Thanks for saving me too. I appreciate it. And, if you ever get the urge to fly with me again, please don't."

"Was I that bad?"

"No, you were fine. It's your penchant for bad luck I'd prefer to avoid."

"Sorry again."

"Not to worry. On the other hand, have you seen the lab's footage of me re-animating your body? It's amazing! I didn't know I could do that."

"No, I haven't seen it."

"You should. It's priceless! Especially the part where I try to walk around in that big, lumbering body of yours."

"I'm sure."

"So Flynn, if that luck of yours ever puts you in a coma again—or even better, if you die—please let me know. I would be happy to zombie you around for a month or so, or at least until you get so ripe they throw you off the ship."

"Thanks, Oscar. You have no idea how much that means to me."

●

CHAPTER 10

THE END

A l is gone," Flynn announced to the Dinner Club. "She left to complete her mission."

"Where?"

"Inward. Closer to the Sun. Her ship's got special features that make it expensive to operate, so she owes a lot to her investors."

"As do we," said Dr. Lonigan. "We owe the University and others. That's why we're going outward."

Carolyn said, "I thought we were shortening our voyage due to the Omega Problem."

"We are. We're stopping the search for debris at Pluto. We'll go as far as that, take some pictures, and wait."

Ernie asked, "Wait? What are we waiting for?"

Lonigan didn't answer at first. Instead, he idly gathered his dishes into a stack. Then he looked around the table. "The truth," he said at last, "is that our government—various governments, in fact—asked us to wait."

"Why?" asked Carolyn.

"Because this Omega thing could be serious." With that, Lonigan picked up his plates and walked away.

Carolyn watched him go. "He doesn't usually do that," she said.

"What?" asked Flynn, "Share information?"

"No," Carolyn answered, "bus his own dishes. Now I'm really worried."

●●●

Flynn looked up at the stars above Pluto. There were so many! And they were sharp and clear. He thought, *This would be a good spot for an astronomical observatory. The stars are even bright on the 'daylight' side. It's perfect…except that it's so darn cold…and so darn remote. Hard to re-supply. The station would have to be automated with remote control, or possibly staffed by robots.*

He was being hosted by his old friend Sela again. She said, "We wouldn't like to staff this place any more than you would."

Had he been thinking out loud? Flynn asked, "Why do you say that?"

"Because it's cold and remote and hard to re-supply."

He had! He said, "Okay, sorry. Remote control then, like deep-space probes."

"I'm glad you agree."

"And I'm glad you invited me to ride along with you today. I don't think I would've gotten to explore Pluto otherwise."

"You wouldn't have."

"Why not?"

"Because none of the other robots wants you to come along with them."

"They don't like me?"

"They like you just fine. They just don't like your luck. Sorry."

"Then why did you allow me to join you?"

"Because, in our colony, we have a code to follow."

"What code is that?"

"83."

"What's that?"

"The code you requested."

"I meant, what does it say?"

"Oh. The words, roughly translated into English, would be something like, 'If you save a machine, then you're responsible for that machine throughout its remaining warranty period.'"

"So…I'm still under warranty?"

"With the colony, yes."

"Then I guess it's a good thing. Thank you for the invitation."

"You're welcome. Just don't mess it up."

"I won't. I'm being careful. And besides, we spiders are extremely tough, so—trust me—nothing can go wrong."

Sela said, "Wait a minute…wait…there has been a general recall of all personnel. This ride-along is cancelled. Please remove your headset."

"Why? What happened?"

"The Sun just exploded."

●●●

The Sun hadn't totally exploded. Professor Lonigan explained the situation when everyone had gathered in the mess hall.

"Ladies and gentlemen," he said, "about an hour ago we detected a large flare on the surface of the Sun. Our telescope confirmed that dwarf planet 23097 Galera had crashed into it. The good news here is that the Sun seems to have absorbed the impact and will probably stabilize. The bad news is that the resulting plume of ejecta appears to be aimed toward Earth. It's large and it's fast. The current estimate is that the ejection mass will hit Earth in another five hours. In the meantime, we're monitoring the news feed, which we're projecting on screens around the ship."

Someone asked, "Shouldn't we go back to help out?"

Lonigan replied, "Yes, we will go back. We'll get as close as we can, assess the damage, and then determine what needs to be done. But don't forget where we are: we're five communication hours away at the speed of light. So what—for us—*will* happen, has—for Earth—*already* happened."

At that, the room went silent.

• • •

They watched the news feed. After an hour or so, Flynn got a text from Louise. She had written, "*It's coming, and nobody can do anything about it. Remember, I will always love you.*" Flynn texted back, "*I love you too, forever,*" but he knew it would never be delivered.

As the hours ticked by, the talking heads on the news feed became more certain that the cloud would be a direct hit. A frequent visual was an observatory's telescopic view of the approaching cloud. It was black and laced with fire. As it got larger, the observatory kept zooming out to keep it in frame. Then they stopped zooming and angry clouds filled the screen. Then they stopped switching to the panelists and stayed with the cloud view. Flynn thought that maybe there was no one left in the network control room to change it. But the announcer's voice went on in the background, describing everything that was happening right up until the end, when the screen suddenly filled with a bright glare…and then nothing.

Carolyn said, "Oh." It sounded like she'd been punched in the gut.

Ernie said, "*But the day of the Lord will come as a thief in the night; in which the heavens shall pass away with a great shout, and the earth and all elements therein shall melt with fervent heat.*"

Flynn said, "That sounds biblical."

Ernie said, "King James, more or less."

No one else in the hall said anything. Instead, they all filed out silently. Flynn walked back to his quarters and sat down. He didn't bother to turn on a light.

●●●

Flynn's phone chimed. The message was, "*I'm so sorry for what happened.*" It was from Al.

Flynn sent, "*Thanks. Where are you?*"

"*I'm outside your door.*"

He opened his door. They fell into an embrace. His tears fell on her torso. Her tears drenched his head.

He thought, *Thank you for coming back.*

She thought, *I had to return.*

Did you see it?

That was my mission: to observe, to record, and to analyze. I did.

It's such a tragedy! Such a waste of human beings! I don't know…I don't think I can deal with it.

They sent me here because I'm a good scientist. I'm careful in obser-vation, meticulous in recording, and dispassionate in analysis.

Good for you.

I've been here for a long time, watching Earth, and now I've filed what may be the only official report of its demise.

What did you say?

A lot of good science. But in the end, I wrote that humanity got what it deserved.

Flynn broke the embrace. "That was a bit cruel," he said.

Click. Click. Click. Flynn looked at the translation: *It was accurate. It was cruel. I apologize.*

Flynn said, "I don't think I'm the right person to accept your apology."

Click. *No, you're not.* Click. *But I'm here to also apologize to you personally.*

"For what?"

Click. *I'm very aggressive about gathering scientific data.* Click. *Perhaps I'm too aggressive.*

"How?"

Click. *I saw your ship and knew what it was.* Click. *I came aboard to learn more about your culture.* Click. *And to trick you into giving me your samples.*

"You tricked me?"

Click. *I didn't have to.* Click. *Wendell Rose did that for me.* Click. *But I accepted it.* Click. *I'm sorry.*

"Oh, don't be. I didn't mind so much. In fact, I enjoyed meeting you, and…I thought we were friends."

Click. *That's the problem.*

"What? That I'm not allowed to make friends with your

species?"

Click. *No.* Click. *That I'm not allowed to make friends with yours.* Click. *But I did.*

"You did?"

Click. *Yes.* Click. *We are friends.* Click. *And now I'm going to break the rules for you.*

"How?"

Al reached out and took him by the arm. *Come with me.*

"Where?"

To my ship.

"Why?"

Because my ship has a special design. It can navigate Minkowski space.

"But that's just physics terminology. It doesn't really…it's…oh!"

●●●

Louise sat in her apartment, watching the news reports. She searched for the remote, found it, and clicked the mute button. The menacing cloud—the end of the earth—remained on screen. All around her, people in their apartments were doing apartment things. People in the street were doing street things. Her door was double-locked and chained.

She picked up her phone. She sent a text to Flynn, "*It's coming, and nobody can do anything about it. Remember, I will always love you.*"

Her screen bubbled for a moment, and then the words, "*I love you too, forever,*" popped up.

She typed, "*Who is this?*"

"*It's me.*"

"*Where are you?*"

"*On the roof.*"

"*Get down here! Now!*"

"*I'll be right there.*"

She opened the door, and they fell into each other's arms. After a long moment she said, "I thought you were on Pluto."

"I was. But it's not very nice this time of year."

"You should have stayed."

"I decided I'd rather be here. A friend was coming this way, so I hitched a ride."

"I wish you hadn't, but since you did…take your clothes off."

"Why?"

"So we can spend the rest of our lives in bed together."

"That's a good idea. But I have a better one."

"What?"

"Let's run away and get married."

"That's a good idea too. But how can we?"

"A ship's captain can marry us, and I know two of them."

"I mean, how can we run away?"

"Oh. My friend Al is parked on the roof. She's got her own spaceship."

"Is that the lady with the tentacles?"

"Yup. But don't worry. After you get to know her, you won't even notice them. I think you two will like each other."

"We'll see."

"In the meantime—and we don't have a lot of it—let's pack a bag for you: comfortable clothes, lots of underwear, and all the photos we've got." He helped her pack and escorted her to the elevator.

She asked, "Why do we have to go off with some alien? Can't we just…I don't know…go down to the basement and ride it out there?"

"Because the earth will be destroyed completely. There won't be anything left: no buildings, no basements, and no atmosphere. Trust me. I saw it."

"Wait a minute. You saw it?"

"Umm, yes."

"And now you're here?"

"Yes."

"Is this some kind of joke?"

"No. This is a special favor from Al, who's breaking her laws to do this."

"What laws?"

"The ones against interfering with other species. She brought me here to rescue you, and that's a serious violation. Let's not let her gesture go to waste."

"Is this some sort of 'alternate universe' thing?"

"No. It's her spaceship. It's designed to navigate Minkowski space."

"What's that?"

The elevator opened. They rode it up to the top floor. When they opened the door to the roof, they heard strange sounds from all over the city. The night sky was beginning to glow with light from the approaching cloud. And there was Al's very alien-looking ship.

Flynn said, "Minkowski space is not just the three dimensions of space we're used to. It's the three dimensions of space and the fourth dimension of time combined."

"Oh, that," she said. "You're talking about the spacetime continuum."

"Yes. How did you know?"

"I read about it in *Popular Science.* In an article on time travel."

"Oh. I guess I missed that issue."

"Then I hope you're not driving."

"No, I'm not. Al is. But she has some rules we have to follow."

"Such as?"

"Umm, remember how you wanted me to take my clothes off downstairs? Well, now we're both going to have to take ours off to get on board."

"So, what is this thing…a party ship?"

"No, but it's a bit like a swimming pool…only without water."

"Where everybody gets naked? Just what is it you and Al have been doing in there?"

"I told you. I've got this thing for tentacles."

"Not anymore," she said.

CHAPTER 11

DECISIONS

Earth was due to pass out of the ejecta plume in three days. During that time the Day Pro returned and waited for it to emerge. Life aboard was frantic with preparations for rescue, searching the communication bands for any survivors' signals (there were none), and providing a news feed to the Lunar and Martian bases.

Earth came out of the fire totally changed. There were no oceans. There was no atmosphere. The surface that remained was only a charred ember. The Day Pro searched long and hard anyway but detected no survivors. After two days, the calls for help from the Moon were too urgent to ignore any longer.

The Lunar bases had been better prepared than Earth for the impact. They were already living below ground and without an

atmosphere. Still, damage had been done to all the surface facilities and even a few below the surface. There were casualties, and
those were evacuated first. The Day Pro spent the next ten days
loading the remaining survivors and as much of their supplies as
they could salvage.

•••

Carolyn Parks came to Dinner Club wearing baggy sweats. She
sat down wearily and put her head in her hands. She wore no
makeup, and her hair hung down around her face.

Al asked, Click?

"I'm okay," Carolyn said. "I've just been volunteering in the
medical bay. I'm a little tired, is all." She moved her head from
side to side. "And my neck is sore."

"Excuse me." Ernie got up from the table and picked up his
dishes, then Al's. He walked away.

Al said, Click.

Carolyn said, "Thanks, Al. I appreciate it. I think all I need is
a little food…and a lot of sleep."

"May I touch your shoulders?"

Carolyn looked around. Ernie had come back and now stood
behind her. "Yes. Sure…I guess."

Ernie put his hands out and placed them on either side of her
neck.

Carolyn said, "Ohh…umm…where'd you learn to do that?"

Ernie said, "I don't know. It's just something I'm good at."

Carolyn said, "Well…you've got an hour to cut that out."

Ernie said nothing. He just continued to focus on her for a
long while.

When he finished, Carolyn put a hand over his, smiled, and said, "Thanks."

•••

The passengers formed a Planning Committee to decide what to do next. Some wanted to return to Earth and start rebuilding. The consensus was that it wouldn't be possible to rebuild, especially with no atmosphere. Others wanted to rebuild civilization on the Moon. Recent evacuees from the lunar bases persuaded them not to. At that point the Committee decided to table the discussion and move on to Mars.

The Martian bases welcomed the Day Pro crew. The Planning Committee moved down to the surface and continued its debate. Some people proposed establishing expanded bases there on Mars, but calculations presented by the Martians confirmed that there weren't enough resources to do it. That left searching beyond the solar system as the only option. But where?

Various candidate systems were proposed, but none were agreed on. In the end, it was Wendell Rose who helped provide the answer.

Wendell stood up in the meeting and cried, "You idiots! We know there are habitable systems out there! There's your proof!" He pointed at Al. "Make it tells us where that is. We can go there. We can negotiate for a parcel of land of our own. If not, we can use more forceful means of negotiation. But make it tell! Make it tell!"

Al said, Click.

Professor Lonigan, who headed the Committee, said, "The Chair recognizes the representative from the planet Beautiful."

Al stood up. In fact, she rose to her full two point five meters and stood there, silently, for a long moment. Then she vomited on Wendell Rose.

Wendell said, "Gahhh!"

Al reached down and retrieved an angry red globe from the mess. She held it high above her head and said, Click. *This is my death!* Click. *I will release it inside of me before revealing the location of my home!*

Professor Lonigan said, "That response is not exactly according to Roberts' Rules of Order...but we'll accept it."

He looked around the room and continued, "Al makes a good point. Nobody—that is, no alien civilization—would want us to come to their neighborhood. I don't think we'd want to, either. That makes us refugees. We need to find a new place of our own."

This was followed by a hubbub around the room. Finally, Al raised a tentacle. Professor Lonigan banged his gavel and said, "Yes Al?"

Al said, Click. *This ship is ancient.* Click. *This ship is your answer.* Click. *It knows where unexplored space lies.*

Finally, after consultation with the ship, the robots, and the astronomers, and after much further debate, they agreed to head off toward two nebulae in the Perseus Arm. On the charts, they were named "Heart" and "Soul," respectively. The choice was only semi-scientific: the ship assured them that the Perseus Arm was unexplored, and Captain Wagner had fond memories of playing that tune on his parents' piano.

* * *

The evacuation of the Martian bases took nearly three weeks. After that, the Day Pro moved out to Triton, where a robot named Oscar helped to set up a tunnel system to refill the ship's reservoirs from a triangular cenote there. Captain Wagner was at first reluctant to bring alien water aboard, but Cyrus assured him that Day Pro's decontamination system was already capable of purifying the water. In fact, it had done so previously, in many similar situations.

Finally, the ship was ready. But then it hesitated.

•••

Captain Wagner called Bosun Schwarz to his office. He said, "We can't just go."

Ernie asked, "Why not?"

"It doesn't feel right. We need something to…to commemorate. We need to set the mood."

"The mood, sir? What are we? A cruise ship?"

"No, but this is serious. It's like standing over a grave and needing to say a few words. It would be wrong not to."

Ernie said, "Sir, do you remember that small matter of discipline I brought to you earlier?"

"Oh, that. Have you decided how to handle it?"

"Yes sir, I have. It will take planning, but we can do it. And…I think it's what we need to do."

•••

Captain Wagner made an announcement over the PA system. "Attention! All hands will lay aft to witness punishment! Umm… that is…all personnel…ah…everybody on board, please come to the town square. We've got a crime to deal with."

Everyone made their way to the square, whispering rumors and bubbling with the first twinges of excitement. When they were gathered, Captain Wagner stood up.

He said, "As you know, we've got a stowaway on board. She was sneaked in by a member of the Bosun Crew. Therefore, on the recommendation of Bosun Schwarz, we've decided to impose the stiffest possible penalty. In fact, it's a life sentence…so please join us in celebrating the marriage of Flynn Prescot Hopper and Louise Diane March!"

The crowd cheered and applauded.

The couple hadn't been able to decide which captain should preside, so they'd asked both to officiate. Al wanted to perform the full Beatific rite, but since that took three days to complete, they opted for a simpler Earth ceremony with a few Beatific elements. Ernie was the Best Man. Carolyn was the Maid of Honor. And Professor Lonigan was the Waterkeeper. (Al assured him it was an esteemed position.)

Captain Wagner opened the ceremony with a formal welcome to all.

Professor Lonigan continued with some wise advice to the couple, and then Al added some traditional words of Beatific. However, when she warned them to avoid Schnilz and Kroots, Flynn suspected she was putting them on.

Finally, Captain Wagner read from his book, the rings were exchanged, and Flynn kissed Louise.

Al said, CLICK!

The couple turned, smiled, and waved to the crowd. The crowd cheered and waved back.

And if, in the next hours, there happened to be cake and punch, singing and dancing, handshakes and hugs, laughter and tears, then all of those things were appropriate.

And if the joy of new beginnings was mingled with the sorrow of great loss, then that was fine too.

Because it's okay to cry at weddings.

EPILOGUE

A lonely, automated telescope on Mars tracked the starship *De Profundis* as it traveled farther away from what had once been a noisy planet.

Somewhere around the orbit of Pluto it paused and seemed to hang in the sky, as though allowing its passengers to look homeward one last time.

Then it suddenly winked out of existence, no doubt plunging outward again, away from the solar system, and back down into the deep from whence it came.

Acknowledgments

I would like to thank the people who've interacted with me throughout a long lifetime. Most of you have loved me, liked me, befriended me, or helped me. Thankfully, only a few of you have done wrong to me. But if you know me, it may just be that you're here. If so, then you've entered the blender of my imagination, been stirred into the mix of my story, and come out with tentacles, green skin, mechanical arms, or whatever —but it's you peeking out of these pages. It was great fun. Thank you!

About the Author

Michael L. Stevens has served as actor, playwright, and co-owner of two theatrical companies specializing in murder mysteries. He has also published cowboy poetry, and mastered the art of wrapping a bullwhip around volunteer tourists in the Colorado Rockies, "fortunately without damage, injury, or lawsuit."

He graduated with honors from Michigan State University, and studied English Literature at the University of Michigan before, as he puts it, "cleverly evading the draft by enlisting in the Army and ending up in a combat zone, where he was shot at without result and returned fire with equal precision."

As a result of his fascination with computers, his "real jobs" have included technical writer, systems analyst, database designer—and Jeep tour guide to the summit of Pikes Peak.

He currently lives with his wife in the Pacific Northwest, but you can connect with him at www.michaellstevens.com and on Facebook at michael.stevens.972663

Falling Through Space is his debut novella.